A Collection of Short Stories
by
Colleen Libby

VOLUME II

The Hole Under the Altar

Copyright © 2020 by Erin Libby

All rights reserved. No portion of this book may be reproduced, stored in a retrieval system, or transmitted in any form or by any means without the prior written permission of the publisher.

ISBN 9780999429624
LCCN 2020917990

First edition.

Printed in the United States of America.

Table of Contents

The Hole Under the Altar 5

The Divorce 17

Charlie's Fence 19

Mission Equivocal 23

Nest Egg 43

After You Win What Then? 53

Never Return A Gift-Horse 63

Once There Were Two Robbers 67

Bugeeshi 87

Animal Shelter 95

Wine of the Country 97

Joint Tenancy 105

Frank 111

Street Car Winter 121

Summer Television 131

The Hole Under the Altar

Now it happened that, just at evening, a young man, sorely beset by hounds, came running across the sodden fields through a pelting rain and behind the hounds came two sheriff's deputies with guns.

The running man feared that, as darkness closed down and weariness shortened their tempers, his pursuers might simply shoot him and go home to supper. He, therefore, ran with all his might toward the steeple of the church of St. Jean the Pardon Master, which he could see beyond a thicket of plum.

And the running man had a great need of pardon, for, as he was penniless and hungry, he had robbed a merchant who kept a fine store at a crossroad, although, it being a Sabbath, the merchant was, as yet, unaware of his loss. But the two sheriff's deputies, abroad on official errands, chanced to hear the rending of the lock and so it came about that the thief, carrying a bag filled with such viands as he had been able to snatch in passing, was fleeing from the officers and their dogs.

Now, the man grew faint, for he had been ill with an affliction of his left hand and had only this day left the hospital. He began to stagger and must surely have been overtaken, but that a little crock of hare's meat, preserved in herbs and vinegar, burst from the straining sack and smashed on the small stones awash among the roots of the rain-flattened grass.

Then the dogs were greatly confounded and they splashed about in the pungent-smelling water, complaining and calling their masters, and their quarry was thus able to pass through the thicket and gain the church.

The church, crudely built and ineptly ornamented, was a tiny place that could not have held, all at one time, the two hundred souls who lived in the village around it. This shortcoming was of no consequence to the villagers, who had erected the building, not for religious use, but as a monument to their stubbornness and to the tenacity of their belief in the truth of their native lore. Besides, they had no pastor nor priest among them.

The fugitive was dismayed to find, upon entering the church, that it had no furnishings of any sort, save only a narrow altar on a dais and, in the back wall, a small empty shrine made of smooth stones and bits of tile and colored glass.

Having a dread of being pulled down by the hounds and disappointed at finding the place so bare, the man would have, then and there, surrendered himself to the deputies, save that he thought he could see a light shining between the floorboards behind the altar. When he approached the spot, the light vanished, but he could smell the tallowy smoke of a snuffed candle.

Taking no thought for what might lie beneath, the man lifted the loosened boards and dropped into the cavity under the dais, believing, no doubt, that his plight could in nowise be worsened. He fell farther than he expected and only by wrapping both arms around the splitting sack was he able to keep a grip on the prize for which he had risked his freedom.

Very close by, someone lifted a broken, clay pot, which had served as a candle shield, and the burning candle was used to ignite another. In the light, the thief saw that he was in a small cell, no bigger than a large closet, scooped neatly from the earth beneath the altar. Vestments hung from pegs driven into the earthen wall and there was a roll of bedding in the corner.

The occupant of the cell, a stout, bald man, had appropriated the only stool and was sitting with a wide board across his knees. In his hand he held a writing pen. The candles were stuck to the two upper corners of his board. The bald man smiled at the thief in a friendly way, but his ruddy face wore an aspect of greed.

"I smell meat!" he cried, "and pickle! I hope you have a generous heart.

"There is enough and to spare," the thief answered, "but since you look somewhat roomy in the midriff, I shall measure the portions myself. What are you writing?"

"A diploma from a famous college," the stout man answered and he showed the thief a divided box containing all manner of inks and pens and papers, some tinted and some handsomely embellished, with seals upon them.

"I sell prestige," he said," and position. There is a worthy young man in this village and, in the next, a school wanting a teacher. My certificate will bring them together and the young man will make me a little gift of money from time to time,"

From his pocket he drew out a copybook, seemingly written by many hands and, on the diploma, he skillfully duplicated the signature of the Dean of a famous college.

When the signature was dry and the certificate returned to its box, the thief took the board upon his own knees and laid out a butt of ham, a slab of cheese, a loaf of bread and such other dainties as he had swept into his sack.

As he drew out his knife to serve the repast, they heard a scraping at the floorboards above their heads and looked up to see a gnomish old face hanging in the hole, watching them.

Quick as a cat, the forger darted up and, laying hands on the old fellow, forced him to come down into the little chamber.

The old man's priestly cloak and hat were soaked with rain and, with an apologetic smile at his captors, he removed these garments and hung them, dripping, on the pegs, all the while eyeing the food with longing. The two who had first arrived were amazed to see that, underneath, he wore clothes of sprightly color and had a red kerchief about his neck.

By way of invitation to join them, the thief brushed crumbs from one end of the board, clearing a small space for the newcomer. The little man nodded and, pushing aside some of the vestments, revealed a deep niche dug into the wall. He reached in and drew out a jug of wine and some cups. Whereupon, they all sat upon the ground around the board and ate and drank with much enjoyment.

While the hidden men were thus diverting themselves, they heard the thumping feet of the deputies in the church above them. Immediately, they covered the candles and waited in silent anxiety. But the policemen, not liking to bring dogs into the church, left them to whine and snuffle outside.

When the searchers had gone away again, the three underneath the altar had honey cakes and wine to celebrate.

"I take it this is your hidey-hole," the forger said to the old man. "Are you a preacher?"

"Well, yes and no," the old man answered. "I studied many years at a seminary, but I was ever a shy man and when it was time for me to take a church of my own, I had not the arrogance to accept it. I asked for and received permission to enter a monastery."

"Coward!" chided the stout man in his friendly way.

"Exactly!" the old man said. "The subdued life I led among the brethren suited me well, but it intensified the flaws in my character. A timid man should wear brave clothes and have commerce with many strangers, so that he ceases to shrink from new eyes and new judgments. So, I left my safe refuge and went about the land, doing such things as might combine the discipline of audacity with the penance of regret. But I still love churches. Hence, my little cell here where I am at home whenever I come this way."

The forger laughed. "I see! You became a charlatan and a trickster!"

"Perhaps I did," the old man said, "but I gained enough courage to act as shepherd to a small flock of my own. I wish, now, that I could return to the church."

He reached into the niche and found fresh candles. When they flared at first lighting, it was plain to see that the man who had provided the meal was unwell.

"Here, now, what's wrong with you?" the forger asked.

The thief displayed a hand swaddled in damp bandages.

"I had a finger amputated this morning. just the first two joints. It was black with poison and the pain was past belief." He forced himself to sit more straightly. "Well," he said, "the finger is gone and it won't grow back. What manner of church is this?"

"It's not a real church," the old man answered. It's a testament to the faith of the folk hereabout in the teachings of their fathers."

He stood against the wall and, clasping his hands as though they rested on a lectern, addressed his listeners in the stately language that had shaped his youthful mind and rendered him unfit for work of an ordinary sort.

"It came to pass that one, reputed to be a great scholar, came among the villagers and he journeyed abroad by day, digging amongst the weed and bramble and seeking speech with the elders and, also, with outlanders living at a distance, who knew little of the ways of this place.

"And when he had done these things, he spake unto the people saying: 'Your village of St. Jean the Pardon Master is misnamed, for, verily, no such saint ever lived.' And he said further that their St. Jean, a great healer, known to converse with animals, was, in truth, an immigrant Fleming called Jan, the <u>Paarden Meester</u>, that is to say, Jan the horse master. This Jan, he said, was but a veterinarian and a blacksmith, whose forge lay in ruin under the saplings on the riverbank. And he denied that many who were troubled had come from afar, even traveling by night, to beg from the saint the holy runes with which he cured them.

"Then the people were wroth with the scholar and might have fallen upon him, but he, being prudent though misguided, arose in all haste and went out from this place while it was yet dark."

"Then the people brought together all things that were needful: stones and mortar and boards, even windows of glass, and they raised up here a tangible refutation of him who would divest their saint of his name and his power."

The churchman sat down on the roll of bedding, blushing with pleasure at the murmured applause of the forger and the thief.

The stout man drew out of his box a document elaborately lettered on vellum, and he asked, "Do you think that, if you were their spiritual leader, the people here would use their church and do homage to their saint?"

"Be assured they would," the little man answered, "but I lack the credentials."

The forger smiled. "You are just now being ordained. What name shall I put down as yours here in the place for it?"

"Victor," the old man said. "For a timorous man, the name has a fine, triumphant sound to it."

The forger completed the document and, searching in his copybook, affixed a mighty signature.

The old man, wiping away happy tears, accepted the scroll and asked, "What do you want in exchange?"

"This hidey-hole," the forger answered. "From time to time I have need of a place where I am known and welcome. Now that the church is yours, the hole shall be mine."

They divided the last of the wine to toast the old man's ordination.

"And what do you want, my friend?" the bald man asked, turning to the thief. "A pardon?"

"I think a forged pardon will scarcely serve me," said the thief. "not with so many of the sheriff's minions at this moment searching the by-ways and hedges for me."

"What was your crime?"

"Improvidence!" the thief answered bitterly. "I have eaten more stolen bread than ever I paid for, because I could never learn the knack of keeping body and soul together on the money that came to hand. I have been in prison many times and the place I ran away from this morning was the prison doctors' surgery."

"A new identity might be more congenial to your needs."

The thief held out his damaged hand. "A thing hard to encompass with this to betray me."

The forger shook his head. "Tell him, Victor, that all granted wishes have their provenance in faith," he said, as the thief fell backward in a swoon, sleeping with his legs still crossed like a tailor's.

"Did you put a drug in his wine?" the old man asked in a quaking voice.

"That I did," the forger said, lifting the divided tray out of his box. In the compartment underneath lay strips of washed linen, sutures, medicaments and surgical tools encased in clean cloths.

While the old man watched, appalled but calm, the forger unwrapped the thief's hand, disclosing the stump of the third finger on his left hand. Quickly he smeared the hand of the sleeper with a strongly aromatic ointment and, with the expedition of one used to dehorning the furious bull, he snipped off two joints of the man's fourth finger, so that it matched the third. In minutes, the new stump was cleansed, sutured and coated with a healing paste. When he had wrapped the hand in a fresh dressing, the forger straightened the thief's legs and covered him with vestments taken from the wall.

While the old man went to sit beside their unconscious companion, the forger addressed himself to the manufacture of documents, both large and small. When he had finished, the man who had fallen insensible to the ground as a thief with one finger missing had become an honest man, lacking two.

When the thief awoke and learned what had been done, he was not altogether pleased, but when he assessed the weight of his little finger against the weight of the time still to be spent in prison, he was not altogether displeased either.

"Tonight, when the young teacher comes for his diploma," the forger said, "you can ride in his cart to the next town. There, he will take you to a stall where some young monks will be selling meal and dried lavender. Since you are now a lay brother of their order," he continued, offering one of his forgeries to the thief, "and, since their Superior is known to me," he said, adding a letter closed with a seal, "they will take you with them to their monastery, and Brother, in that frugal and industrious community, you will be cured of your improvidence!"

The thief laughed aloud and, rising weakly, wrapped himself in one of the robes and tucked his crossed hands into the wide sleeves.

"What do you want in exchange?" he asked.

"A trifle, which I have already taken. The finger."

"Keep it and welcome," said the thief. And the others made him sit to rest on the bedding, while the forger measured together, into an empty wine cup, powders and elixirs from among his medicines. When the mixture fumed, he dropped the finger in and set the cup aside. Already, the finger had begun to shrivel and darken.

"I would not like the young teacher to know of this hole," the forger said, packing up his box. "We must meet him in the church above, according to my agreement with him."

In the box, he came upon a little silver casket filled with blotting sand. This he emptied upon the ground and, handing the casket to the old man, said, "When the fluid is entirely evaporated from the cup, put the finger in here."

"Why?" the old man asked.

"For a relic! The good people here deserve a relic of their saint."

The new made priest looked embarrassed and reluctant.

"How shall I say I came by it?" he asked.

"In your place, I should say I got it from the saint, himself," the forger replied.

He reached up and shifted the floorboards. Then, having stationed the thief under the opening, he clasped him strongly about the knees and raised him until he could sit on the church floor at the edge of the hole. Next, he handed up his box and, seizing the rim of the hole, sprang vigorously upward and drew himself into the church.

Then the forger and thief lay on the floor with their heads thrust into the little cell to bid farewell to the old man, who had seated himself on the stool and, trammeled by indecision, was tossing the silver casket from hand to hand. They could hear cart wheels churning the mud of the roadway.

The thief looked at the forger's friendly face, shining red in the candlelight, and said to the old man, "Victor, how can you know of a certainty that what our companion tells you to say is untrue?"

The old man smiled sweetly at the thief, but spoke to the forger. "It may be true enough, Master, but I am hard-put to devise an answer for the time when my flock shall ask me how the name, 'Jan' came to be engraved on the bottom of the casket."

The Divorce

We climbed all day, my wife and I, up craggy paths and spiky scrub, before we came out on the mountaintop, just after sundown and saw my mother-in-law's hut. I stood against a sky striped in thousand-mile bands of smoky red and black, as if someone had started a brush fire in heaven.

I stopped Estella when we were a few yards from the house and called out, "Sorceress! Witch! I've brought your daughter back to you!"

We heard footsteps in the cabin and I turned my back to the open door so I should not see the old woman's evil eye. "I renounce her utterly," I called out. "In two years she has not conceived. She cannot cook, or milk a goat, or even wash a pot.

All she does is sing with the birds, dance with the wind and follow the flock. She is beautiful, but useless and I do not want her!"

I had expected screeches and curses from the mother, but she said kindly, "I accept her. Go in peace. "My wife laid her soft little hand on my arm in a gesture of farewell. "It was good of you to see me home," she said.

I was embarrassed then and, to make amends for my discourtesy, I said over my shoulder, "you must understand, Witch, that I did my best, but beating her taught her nothing, starving her taught her nothing, even locking her out to sleep on the hills taught her nothing. What more could I do?"

Unthinkingly, I turned in apology toward the hut and looked fully in the old woman's face. She stood in the doorway on wide-braced feet, like a red-eyed condor, with her black shawl-ends flapping and the dreadful sky staining her features.

I was so vexed by my own carelessness that I needed something to repair my self-esteem. I captured my wife's hand and jerked the heavy gold ring from her finger. The ring was a peculiar thing with a little bird-headed God incised in it, but it was too small for me, so I dropped it in my shirt pocket.

I threw it away on the downward trail, because it seemed to burn my chest, but even after it was gone my chest burned and the vultures followed me, though most of the journey was made in darkness. They are on the roof now, but I have not the strength to get out of bed and throw sticks at them.

Charlie's Fence

Last year Charlie's fence was new. Each slender, six-foot paling abutted firmly against the next to form a claustrophobic wall of fresh, rosy wood, thirty yards long and chink-less.

We were glad that Charlie built the fence, for we have symbol bushes growing in the long ribbon of earth we call our garden. The garden, lavishly watered and seldom pruned, is packed with green mementoes of Mother's Days, Easters, Christmases and birthdays gone by. There we have transplanted sprigs of nameless plants pilfered on happy excursions, and bits of herbage begged from neighbors and complete strangers. Our handsome little rubber tree was rescued as a starving foundling from a trash can.

In the days before the fence, it was Charlie's habit to whack off every tentative tendril that ventured above the low retaining wall that protected him from our ever growing past. Sometimes, in the vigor of his distaste, he uprooted whole sections of our lives and threw them out; for Charlie cannot bear the sight of blade, nor leaf, nor any tiny scrap of green growth.

The fence is a guard rail around his spruce house which rests, ship-like, on a deck of barren cement surrounding the place completely, except for a couple of spots where bushels of redwood chips have been spread beneath the riser-less steps. He will have nothing on board except the sun.

Charlie is in love with the sun. He woos it, dressed in crumpled white shorts and a housepainter's cap. He pursues it in a small expensive boat. He lures it into his stifling rooms through narrow celestory windows that will not open.

But the sun does not love Charlie. It cannot penetrate the miasmic overcast in which he has his being. It cannot penetrate the heat without light. It pounds the scorching deck in frustration. It strafes his house in an effort to get into his darkened head. It squeezes his fence.

Dear Lord, what the sun has done to Charlie's fence! Last year's satiny palings are ribbed and corded like long clouts of wrung out linen. Wide apertures are appearing every three inches. Knots are starting like bungs from their holes. In the cross light of evening the fence has an accordion pleated look to it, and is soiled by syrupy droplets of sweat pressed out by the day long grip of the sun. Even the rusting nails are being inexorably drawn out.

We do what we can with stakes and string to keep our verdant memoirs to ourselves, but already a bygone Christmas and a few small anniversaries are sprouting among the redwood chips. I wish we could do something about Charlie's fence.

Mission Equivocal

Joe Carpenter found the fallen angel just at sunup on a tender May morning. He had made his first mug of coffee in the arbor, then carried it outside, as he had done most mornings of the twenty-five years since his father had given him and Mary the farm as a wedding present. The house, the arbor, the vegetable garden and the garages sat high on a gumdrop hill, and Joe found it gratifying to lean on the stone fence that rimmed his hilltop and let his gaze sweep out and down over his well-managed acres.

He stood so, now, a ruddy man, not overly tall, with talkative gray eyes set in a quiet, listening face. His dark hair was heavily threaded with white, but as yet, showed no signs of thinning and his forearms, resting on the fence, were strongly muscled and young looking.

As the sun climbed out of a tangle of trees, he sensed that something was askew and scanned his orderly domain until he discovered that the lightning rod on his barn was broken midway up the stem with the upper half canted toward the house. The glass ball near its tip dangled like a crystal teardrop. Joe left his cup on the fence and went to investigate.

The angel was lying unconscious on the ground, his mighty wings spread wide and soiled with scraps of hay and flakes of dried manure. The rumpled inner feathers blew helplessly in the mild morning breeze.

Joe felt an immediate dislike for the thing. It was large; between six and seven feet tall. The hair fell in a golden cascade over the barnyard dirt, and the skin had the warm whiteness of magnolia blossoms. Joe couldn't tell if the creature was a he-angel or a she-angel. Its structure was primarily masculine, but the hairless, bulging pectorals looked as if they could, at any moment, lift into proud rondures of mammary magnificence. The creamy belly was softly convex and lacked a navel. The pure oval face and the exquisitely sculptured hands and feet could have belonged to either god or goddess. He flicked a corner of the bunchy loincloth aside and discovered that the crotch was as smooth and featureless as the belly. "Poor devil," he said.

At the sound of Joe's voice, the angel opened sweet senseless eyes, the color of blue morning glories, and searched the sky. His roving glance focused on the lightning rod and he asked, cello-voiced, "Where did you get that thing? I thought nobody used them any more."

"Hardly anyone does," Joe answered. "My wife buys up old stuff like that at auctions. She says that farming, the way we do it is a dying profession and that farmers like me will soon seem as romantic as troubadours. Can you get up?" He reached out a hand and, with a twinge of disgust, felt the long, ivory fingers grip his own.

Once on his feet, the angel stretched his wings. A few damaged feathers drifted like snowflakes into the weeds along the barn. Joe was impressed. "You must have a twenty foot wingspan there," he said.

"At least" said the angel, shaking his pinions so that an iridescent nimbus danced across their silky expanse.

"Well," Joe said insinuatingly, "I suppose you'll be zooming off to heaven, now that you've got your wind back?"

"Huh-uh, I'm on a mission. I have to speak with your wife." Then, perceiving Joe's terror, he said, "Hey! It's nothing like that! I'm not an angel of death. I'm just a messenger, like Western Union."

"I'm not sure I want you talking to my wife," Joe retorted, undaunted by the expression of divine stubbornness that congealed the beautiful face. "I will speak to her just the same," the angel replied. "It's my mission."

Joe wondered what his chances were of beating hell out of this pig-headed celestial, but was saved from folly by his wife's voice, calling over the fence: "Joe, is that a real angel you're talking to?" and Joe, remembering the unadorned crotch, laughed and answered, "Mary, this is an honest-to-God angel. He wants to meet you."

They crossed the barnyard, skirted a large, humpback Quonset crowded with farm machinery, and came to the ascent up the hill, a rugged stairway with three-foot logs for risers. These were anchored with metal stanchions and the long, uneven landings between them had merely been scraped out of the pebbly earth and packed down by life-times of use. At this season, the steps zigzagged dizzily skyward through a shivering waterfall of wildflowers and coarse grass.

There's a driveway around in front," Joe said, "Might be a little easier walking."

"It doesn't matter," the angel murmured.

"You gonna walk, or fly?" Joe asked, and his belligerence gave a nasty edge to a question he had meant to be jocular.

"I can't take off from here," the angel answered equably, and they climbed in silence, the angel limping rather badly.

Joe, trying again for a hospitable remark, said, "My grandfather was a preacher. When he had the place, this stairway was called 'Jacob's Ladder'. We still call it that sometimes."

"A poor location for a flight with an angel," his companion said, and, though Joe considered the bland comment carefully, he could find no hint of double meaning.

They came out on the hilltop and entered the long arbor that stretched from stairway to house. The end nearest the kitchen had, long ago, been a wash house, but, having been enlarged a number of times over the years, it was now a spacious summer house, screened against flies and pleasantly shaded by young vines and sheets of translucent plastic. A ceramic churn, a metal cream can and a senile sewing machine had been converted to planters, adding charm to the enclosure, which was dominated by a round, yellow table laid with breakfast for two. Beside it Mary stood waiting for them.

In moments of playful affection, Joe sometimes called his wife his "tawny pigeon," his "amber dove", a lovingly apt description of Mary, with her high-breasted little figure, her topaz eyes and rusty hair. She came toward them as Joe said, "Mary, this is the angel. I don't know his name yet."

"Annunzio," said their guest in his heart-lifting voice. I am called Annunzio."

"I am truly happy to meet you, "Mary said. Let me bring another plate. You go ahead, Joe, before your eggs get cold."

The angel laid a restraining finger on her wrist. "There's no point in bringing another plate," he said gently.

"I should have realized," Mary said, her cheeks flushing. "Well, sit down at any rate." She gestured toward a glider upholstered in printed plastic. "Is there anything I can get for you?"

"Yes," said Annunzio, and lifting his wings into a half-spread position, so they could hang over the back of the glider, he seated himself and stuck out a foot, showing Mary the sole. The bottom of his foot looked sore and abraded, and there were small cuts on the reddened skin. "I'm used to walking on clouds," he said.

Mary went to the screen door at the end of the arbor and called, "Miguel!"

Through the kitchen window a young boy's voice answered, "Yes, Mrs. Carpenter?"

"Fill a dishpan with warm water and bring it out here. More coffee, Joe?" She sat at the yellow table and poured coffee for her husband and herself. Joe ignored his and, reaching across the table, grasped Mary's hand warmly. "You're not to worry, Mary, but Annunzio has a message for you." His dislike for the angel deepened as he watched the color drain from his wife's face and a beseeching expression crept into her eyes.

"A message?" Her voice was marred by the harshness of fear.

"Who would send me a message from heaven?"

"There was no signature," said Annunzio, "but I would surmise…"

"Hey, Mr. Carpenter! Would you get the door?"

Joe went quickly to open the door, as if it were better to prolong the unbearable suspense than to learn the insupportable truth. A dark, handsome boy of seventeen came in, carelessly sloshing water from a large, deep pan. "It's for his feet," Joe said, tipping his head in a curt gesture toward the glider and watching, without pleasure, while Miguel eased the pan onto the ancient brick floor. The angel, with an ecstatic sigh, slid his feet into the faintly steaming bath.

Joe, still desperately stretching the moment of reprieve, laid a fatherly hand on the boy's shoulder. "This is our friend, Miguel Sanchez, who plans to be a great anthropologist one day. He's working for us mornings and after school to earn the fee for a field trip to a dig in South Dakota this summer." The babbling speech died away and Joe was paralyzed by panic. Not even to save himself and Mary could he think of anything more to say. "Miguel, this is Annunzio," he muttered helplessly and went back to Mary.

Miguel's intelligent eyes, black and excited, swept like headlights over the angel. He dropped to his knees, bowed his head and studied his interlocked hands from beneath calculating eyelids. When he raised his face, it was glossed by the innocent guile of the very young and very honest.

"Don't get your hopes up, Miguel," Annunzio said. "I must warn you I have very little benevolence."

"You mean you're a hard-hearted angel? Like the one that stands by Eden's gate? Ah, come on!"

"I mean I'm broke. When angels get a job to do, they get paid in benevolence, which they can use to redress wrongs, thwart injustice, and so on, which earns them more benevolence. The tricky part is getting a lot of jobs so that we can stockpile enough benevolence to subsidize a really worthy endeavor. Otherwise, we're reduced to nickle-and-dime stuff, like sending stray dogs home. So don't ask me to let you find Father Adam's bones in South Dakota.

Miguel looked abashed, but sympathetic. "Don't you know a trade?"

"O yes. I'm a chorister. A long time ago we had these splendid choirs; thousands and thousands of voices. We sang to the shepherds, we sang glad tidings, and we sang for joy. But the traffic noise, the planes, the dwindling interest in a cappella music, and the general preference for sportscasts and weather reports ultimately put most of us out of work. Swarms of angels were transferred to Communications

Hope bloomed in Miguel's face as he tried to work a small notebook and pencil out of his shirt pocket, but it died again when he found the morning glory eyes watching his fingers.

He said defensively, "Well, it wouldn't be much trouble for you just to hand a note to somebody in the right department."

Annunzio leaned forward and effortlessly lifted Miguel to his feet. "Get off your knees, before you cripple yourself. I'm not in Receiving. I'm in Transmitting, the poorest paid job in the Heavenly Kingdom. This is my first mission in nearly two thousand years."

Mary, sitting over her cooling coffee, whimpered, and Joe, to cover the sound, said, "Miguel, you'll be late for school."

"That's right," Miguel answered, uncaring. "I gotta go by home and tell Mom about Annunzio. She's crazy about church and all that religious stuff. If she finds out there was an angel here and I didn't tell her, I'd never see South Dakota."

After the screen door slammed, Joe, watching Annunzio defiantly, said to Mary. "Go on to work, if you want to, hon. If you're not here, he can't give you his damned message!"

Annunzio stood up, stepped out of his pan, and looking on Joe with compassion, he laughed. A clangor of bells seemed to roll the morning sky and a moving radiance flickered through the summerhouse, as a seaside cave is sometimes lighted for a moment by reflections from the swinging ocean.

Mary, rising, said hesitantly, "I hope you won't think us crass, or materialistic, or anything like that, but I have this farm implement agency in town and the Schwartz brothers are coming in before noon to talk about a hay baler. Some years the farm doesn't pay for itself, you know, and we need what I make at the agency to keep it running. I really should go."

"Why not?" asked Annunzio. "The news will keep, and we have lots of time. Low altitude flying is risky before nightfall."

Mary escaped from the arbor, but once outside, she stopped short and leaned around the door jam, her lion-colored eyes glaring at the angel. "It's an insufferable invasion of privacy," she cried. "It's plain, boneheaded despotism? Do you realize that I'm almost forty-five?"

Joe was not surprised. He had, before now, seen his amiable Mary slowly kindled by injustice into a flaming rage, but Annunzio's clear countenance was misted fleetingly by a breath of dismay, then it brightened again as he said, "You'll feel differently, Mary, after you hear the message. Whenever I've been on these missions before, the ladies were rapturous with joy, even the one that was about your age."

Mary pulled her head out of the doorway and slammed the screen in exasperation. "That was B.C.!" she snapped. Before the whole world learned the consequences of listening to you."

She marched, a militant partridge, into the garage where she forced her tired old Plymouth through its morning maneuvers and disappeared down the looping drive that would bring her eventually to the county highway.

"She'll see!" Annunzio assured Joe with angelic optimism. Joe threw him an I-dare-you look and said, "I've got work to do in the barn."

As Joe retreated down the sun-stippled arbor toward Jacob's Ladder, Annunzio composed himself somewhat awkwardly on the glider and fell sweetly asleep.

* * *

While Joe was cleaning an old shotgun in the barn, Consuela Sanchez was holding a brief, but fervid, exchange with her beloved son, Miguel. As soon as she had packed him off to school, she stepped around the corner to discuss with Father Escoto, in his potting shed, the incidence of heavenly visitation as compared to drug-induced hallucination. Protected by a plastic chemists' apron, he gave her the assurance she needed, as he separated seedlings and transferred them to pots. The minute she was gone, he yanked off his apron and treated Mr. Wooten, Miguel's high school principal, to a telephonic tirade on drug traffic in the public schools. He discoursed on the Carpenters, the angel and Miguel, and ended by stating hotly that he would not stand by and let a bunch of teen-age drug-peddlers ruin the lives of fine people like Connie Sanchez and her son.

Wooten, overworked, understaffed and fretted by a hundred problems not even remotely related to his chosen profession of educator, called Miguel into his office. The principal (his mind still occupied by an imaginary rebuttal to Father Escoto's accusations) completely misconstrued the boy's effervescence, his vivid description of Annunzio's presence, and his exuberant belief that the angel might do him some tremendous favor after being paid for his current mission.

"Tell me, once more, Miguel. What was the foreign fellow doing at the Carpenter place?"

"He's not that kind of a foreign fellow, Mr. Wooten. He's an angel, a real angel. He came as a courier, but I don't know what he brought with him. I've already told you!"

"Could you identify him, if you were asked to?"

One whoop of astonished laughter exploded from Miguel's open mouth, before he closed it and got to his feet. "Mr. Wooten," he said as courteously as he could, we're not on the same wave length. You ask the questions, but you're too shot-out to tune into the answers. Would you come with me to the farm and meet Annunzio? You'd have to ride buddy on my motorbike, unless we take your car."

Wooten stared at Miguel, but his tired eyes saw only the probable headlines resulting from such a visit: LOCAL SCHOOL MAN IN CAHOOTS WITH DOPE KING. He, too, spoke as courteously as he could. "Miguel, you little sneak, if you're trying to jockey me into position for blackmail, it won't work. Get out of here and, on your way out, ask my secretary to get you an appointment with the county school psychiatrist."

"She isn't here today, Mr. Wooten," Miguel said as he carefully closed the door.

The principal lifted his telephone and grimly directed the student at the switchboard to get him Police Chief Blankenship.

Clyde Blankenship, a cool man, not much given to riding into battle under transitory banners, listened without reaction to Wooten's opening complaint about the ease at which drug dealers made their way to school ground pushers, and to his oblique hints at police cooperation. The chief was a shade more interested when Wooten got around to the Carpenters, Annunzio-the-Angel, and Miguel.

"Well, that's the story," the principal finally concluded. "The boy didn't make too much sense, but he could have been high on something. Whatever is going on at the Carpenter farm will have to be stopped, Clyde."

Clyde said he'd see to it, and called an old friend in Immigration. "Leland," he said, "Mary Carpenter was in here this morning, asking how to get an unwelcome visitor evicted from her place. Wouldn't tell me much about him. Just said she didn't know the guy and wanted him out of there before she went home to lunch. Acted a little too cagey, I thought."

"So?" asked Leland Bragg. "Where do I come in?"

"A kid that works for the Carpenters says he's positive this visitor had no papers or luggage. Not even any shoes. The dude's name is Annunzio."

"Sounds like mafia."

"Could be. Seems he slipped in during the night and met Joe in the barn about daylight. The kid claims this Annunzio is an extra-terrestrial, but he was stoned to the gills when he was interviewed."

"Oh, hell!" Bragg groaned. "Narcotics too!" How did Joe and Mary ever get into a thing like that?"

"I'd like to find out, but the farm is outside my bailiwick. I've been trying to reach the County Sheriff ever since Mary left."

"Cotton Sonderman? I can see him from where I'm sitting. He's over at the Courthouse Café eating pie. I'll give him the word and get on out there myself. You want to come?"

"I guess not. Thanks anyway."

* * *

Joe Carpenter sat in his barn with the useless shotgun across his knees. "Must have been used for a crowbar," he thought. He heard a car and wondered dimly why Mary was parking in the barnyard, but he remained seated, immobilized by the enormity of their predicament. When he decided that the decrepit gun could never be fired again, he had roved about the barn, selecting and discarding alternative weapons, a pitchfork, a sickle, a pruning knife, a mallet, until it became clear to him he was not going to kill anybody, not even Annunzio; not even if he had a brand new gun. He was so depressed by his fatal squeamishness that he could give the sheriff very little attention when he burst into the barn and waited alertly behind a drawn pistol, while two deputies came up on either side, seized the shotgun, and applied handcuffs with considerable expertise. "Hi, Cotton," was all he could manage, before he sank into a black well of defeat.

He was not aware of the officer who approached the sheriff and said, "Leland Bragg's gone on up. He's mad. Says you should have supported Immigration instead of letting an illegal alien get away while you messed around with Joe Carpenter."

"Hell with him," Cotton said indifferently. "Let's get in the car, Joe. I wanta talk to you."

In the arbor, Annunzio waking refreshed, but cramped by his skimpy bed and the restrictive summerhouse, wandered outside in search of freedom. He found a short, grassy slope that leveled into a tree-shaded wood yard.

Leland Bragg, having left his car beside the sheriff's, toiled up Jacob's Ladder. He lept the breakneck stairs at a crouching run and concealed himself behind the gigantic tree that shaded the wood yard. He stood in its reviving shade for some time, getting his wind back and wishing Sonderman would send reinforcements. When none came, he moved carefully around the tree and caught Annunzio in mid-stretch.

The statuesque arms strained upward toward the tips of stupendous wings that were sun-struck to gauzy brilliance along their outer edges. The anomalous torso and polished limbs glowed warmly luminous. The glittering head was thrown back so that the beautiful mouth might open freely in a noble yawn.

"Oh hell!" said Bragg, slinging a hatchet out of his way and sitting down on the chopping block. "Oh God!"

"You have to make a choice," the angel informed him kindly. "You can't expect help from both." The penetrating resonance of the voice made Bragg clutch at his stomach.

"Are you Annunzio?"

"Of course. Were you looking for me?"

For an answer Bragg said, "Damn Clyde Blankenship!"

Annunzio studied Bragg with benign concern. "You look as if you'd been robbed or wronged," he said.

"Do you know what I'm supposed to do?" Bragg yelled, hopping off the chopping block and doing an agitated turkey-trot. "I'm supposed to arrest you as an illegal alien! I'm supposed to hold you in jail until I can make arrangements to return you to your lawful abode!"

They had not heard Mary's car, and learned she was at home only when she came toward them from the garage, accompanied by Miguel, who had hitched a ride. He was carrying a filled paper bag marked, "Chan's Cantonese Carry-out." Mary hesitated when she saw Annunzio, then came warily forward in time to hear him ask Bragg: "Is there some way I can help you? Some very small way?"

Bragg made shooing motions with his hands. "You can get the hell out of here! Disappear! Vanish! I can tell them you were gone when I got here!"

"Mary!" Annunzio said, fastening compelling eyes on her face, "I must tell you…"

"Will you please go?" Bragg still danced his erratic dance. "Before I'm seen talking to you! Before Cotton Sonderman gets here with his gun-happy goons. They'll shoot you for a Martian!"

"Joe!" Mary gasped. "Leland, where's Joe?"

"He's okay," Bragg lied. "He's with Sonderman down at the barn."

Mary, with Miguel at her shoulder, ran along the side of the arbor toward the fence near the top of Jacob's Ladder. Annunzio and a yammering Bragg followed, until Bragg, crazy with anxiety, plowed ahead to see what the sheriff was doing. Miguel dropped back to join Annunzio, who was limping again. "They can't shoot you, can they?" he asked uneasily, then answered himself. "Nah. Who ever heard of a dead angel?"

"Well." Annunzio said, carefully choosing his footing, "I have no ambition to be the first one you ever hear of."

"You're using up all of your benevolence on <u>him</u>," Miguel said accusingly. He nodded toward Bragg and clasped the paper bag against his chest as if to hide a wound. "You're saving your own neck at the same time, of course. So maybe it doesn't count?"

"It counts," Annunzio said as they came up with the other two, and Miguel swung away to hide his face, tragic with first betrayal.

Annunzio touched Miguel's cheek. "It doesn't take any benevolence to tell you that we're standing on a mound, a Mound Builder's mound. There are hundreds of artifacts somewhere under your feet. Talk to Joe about a private dig out here."

"They're coming!" Bragg warned.

From the hilltop viewpoint the two cars in the barnyard looked as squat as pill bugs and, while the anxious group watched, one of the bugs scurried out onto the road that would bring it around the hill and up the twisted front driveway.

"Wait until they're well around the hill," Bragg said to Annunzio, "then take off."

Annunzio lightly mounted the stone fence and stood facing them, a shining symbol of mystic glory, towering against a cerulean backdrop. Bragg, to give him room, drew Miguel and Mary back a little way from the fence. They could hear the mumble of a motor on the lower levels of the driveway.

"Annunzio," Miguel called, "I'm sorry about your pay-check, your benevolence."

"It won't be too bad," Annunzio answered. "I earned quite a lot, one way and another. And there's always the Bee Bee."

"What's the Bee Bee?"

"'Bonus in Benevolence.' Anyone who accepts a mission to this place gets it automatically."

Mary and the angel looked at each other for a moment and the angel said, "Mary!" then shrugged and suggested, "Another day, perhaps?"

Mary wagged her head in a slow, negative motion. "But I want you to know that I'm glad you came," she said.

Miguel, with a joyous face and streaming eyes, sat down on the ground.

"Hurry!" Bragg whispered in a suppressed scream.

Annunzio, turning away from them, spooned air with his wings and, while the rippling grass lapped like water over their insteps and their clothing clung to their skins, he dived down the hillside.

They thought, with horror, that he had fallen, until he arched gracefully up and out, to become a glider, a floating sheet of paper, a tiny lost kite, a random snowflake, then nothing.

Cotton Sonderman and his two deputies jogged toward them from the turnaround in front of the garage, followed by an unmanacled Joe.

"You find anybody up here?" Sonderman asked Bragg.

"No." Bragg seemed about to add something more, but kept quiet and let his cautious glance move from face to face.

Mary ran to Joe and put her arm around him. "He's gone, Joe," she whispered.

Joe guided her away from Bragg and the sheriff until he could lean with her against the fence. "Are you alright?"

"Like always," she answered happily. "What went on in the barn?"

Joe grinned. "I think I was almost arrested for dreaming. Cotton came in and grabbed me. I guess it was for possession of narcotics, because he kept me talking in the car while the deputies confiscated most of my veterinary remedies. Now, he says I fell asleep while I was tinkering with an old bird gun, and he won't have it any other way. Nothing on earth will convince Cotton Sonderman that we had an angel within our gates."

Miguel joined them. "Mrs. Carpenter," he said, jiggling the paper bag, "it's way past noon. Couldn't we have lunch?"

Sonderman, arriving quietly, reached a thick hand over Miguel's shoulder and confiscated the bag of cold food. "Have to take this in for examination," he said, and, trailed by his deputies, went slogging back to his car.

Bragg, apparently trying to avoid the sheriff, moved slowly toward the hillside stairway. Mary caught his hand. Don't go yet, Leland. Stay and have scrambled eggs with us. "Okay," he said, taking his place with them at the fence.

They lingered there a little while, their arms folded on the stone coping, looking at the broken lightning rod with its trembling glass tear.

A not young couple, living in a semi-rural community have an angel as an unexpected guest and, fearing that he is about to announce the coming of a child, possibly a child with a unique destiny, they strive to prevent him from making his announcement and ultimately, with the aid of circumstance and the police, they bid him farewell without ever hearing his glad tidings.

Nest Egg

"I'm Jeannette Herron," I said to the soft-footed assistant who opened the door of Madame Clara's salon. "Has the eight thirty séance started?"

"Not yet, Miss Herron," he said and led me to a seat beside a woman with chipmunk teeth and worried brown eyes.

There was nothing spooky about the antechamber. The cream furniture and the patterned rose carpet gave the place a homey, comfortable look. The several clients who had arrived before me seemed to be ordinary, likeable people.

The chipmunk lady leaned toward me and whispered, "Did you have to pay in advance?" I said I had and she asked, "How much?" I told her I had understood that a hundred dollars was the established fee and she relaxed a little. "That's what I paid," she said, "but it seems an awful lot, and I wondered if we weren't all fools, a thousand dollars worth of fools, but I couldn't think of anything more sensible I might have done. I wanted to talk to my mother about my inheritance and I'd heard Madame Clara was a gifted medium.

I had inherited my mother's money when she died, almost two years ago, and that was the trouble: To me it was still her money. I'd had no difficulty in paying the attorney's fees, the probate fees and the inheritance taxes out of the estate, because I felt that these were really her debts, but when it came to buying anything for myself, like the cottage, for example I found I couldn't do it. A half a dozen times I had gone to the bank, filled out a withdrawal slip, and then tore it up, because I was sure that Mother wouldn't want me to squander her savings on a house so far from town that I could only use it on weekends, and so dilapidated that it would take a lot of money to make it habitable. The floors were corrugated, the windows were stuck forever, and the backyard was a wasteland of stratified growth that had burgeoned and died and burgeoned again, untouched by rake or spade for the last five years. The cottage was on a small, tree-shaded river, with a shaky old boat landing, and I wanted it with all my heart.

I wanted an escape from the hive I lived in. Except for the hall door, my apartment is boxed in on three sides by solid walls. The windows on the fourth side look down, down, down, down into a cramped little courtyard that is dark even at noon. The vista is about as attractive as a mine shaft. I've stayed there because it's close to the lab where I'm chief medical technician, but there's no hope of making a home out of it, and I've never tried.

I wanted that cottage; a place I could grow roses and where my terrier could run without a leash, a place where Charles and I could enjoy the heavenly privilege of wasting time together.

I have, on occasion, been called a "mature woman", which is a euphemistic way of saying that I have to dye my graying hair and sometimes wear support hose. Charles is a pediatrician with six children of his own, ranging in age from crib-size to junior college. After five easy confinements, his wife, a robust and high-spirited woman, shocked everybody by dying suddenly while delivering her sixth baby. When I met Charles, he had finally gotten his household rearranged. His mother's cousin had come to stay and they had hired a nanny, a cook and a resident college boy who was part-time handyman and part-time child watcher.

I had no inclination to become a part of this tribal complex, and Charles didn't want me to. What he needed most from me was surcease from the vexations of his practice and the demands of his clamorous family.

I could just see us dawdling in a boat on the river, sunning ourselves on the dock, or, in cold weather, sipping hot drinks in front of the fireplace. The realtor had told me he had another tentative buyer for the cottage and I dared not disbelieve him. So why couldn't I just give him a down payment?

Because mother had worked so hard for every dime she had saved!! Until I was old enough to go to school, we had a farm. In addition to cooking and cleaning, washing and ironing, Mother would get into overalls and boots and work in the fields or take care of the livestock, because, she said, the farm couldn't support more than just the one hired hand we already had.

After we moved to town, she always had a job of some kind, so she wouldn't have to touch her savings or use the money she got for the farm. Even after she was sixty years old, she was still working: summers at the local cannery and winters at the cafeteria in the high school. She would do anything to earn a few dollars, so she could add something to her bank balance.

I couldn't stop her! After I got out of lab school, I would fly home every three or four months. We squabbled a lot. I used to ask her, "Mother, why do you kill yourself at these slob-jobs when you don't need the money? And she would answer, "I want to see that you're provided for when I'm gone, Jenny." She made me feel like I was a sub-average child who would be a lifelong financial burden, and I sometimes yelled at her, "You know I can take care of myself! I'm a topnotch medical technician and I make a decent salary! Why do you insist on walking five extra blocks to save two cents on a pound of bacon so you can put two cents in the bank for me?"

"You're going to need a nest egg, Jenny," she always said. "You're not a very common-sensical girl and you may be glad of something to fall back on."

To tell the truth, she never paid any attention to me. I would say, "Mother, why don't you get yourself something you will enjoy, a color television set or an air conditioner? Why don't you go to a nice resort, where it's cool, this summer? You can afford it!" She always said, "Those things are a waste of good money, Jenny. It's better to loan it out at interest."

I couldn't give her anything worth having. If a gift I sent her looked expensive, she would return it to me and tell me to get my money back, saying she would rather see me put the cash in the bank. Once, she kept a seventy-five dollar handbag because she didn't know they could cost that much.

So, one day, after working like a stevedore for over forty years, and scrimping and depriving herself so I could have a nest egg, she dropped dead in the ladies room of the high school, without ever getting much out of life.

I was crying a little when Madame Clara's assistant touched my shoulder. "Madame is ready now," he said, and I looked up to see that all the others had gone in ahead of me.

The salon was as pleasant as the waiting room. The effect of white walls, bright cushions and fresh flowers was scarcely lessened by the large, white dining table standing in the middle of the floor. There was no cover on the table. There were no shrouded alcoves, no mysterious cabinets. Guided by the assistant, we took our places in the padded chairs around the table just as Madame came in.

She was a neat, brisk little woman with snowy, short hair and a tidy figure. There was a touch of shyness about her greeting to us, of hoping to be useful in some way, that we were all immediately enamored of her.

As soon as she sat down the lights were dimmed, but not extinguished. In fact, I've eaten in lots of restaurants that were darker. We sat at the table, each of us touching the outspread hands of our neighbors, while Madame murmured what might have been a prayer, or incantation. Though it was more likely a device for divorcing her mind from insistent attention so that she could concentrate on doing whatever it is mediums do. Presently she went into a trance. She didn't faint or groan, just stiffened into glassy-eyed rigidity and, from where I sat across the table, she appeared to have achieved a perfect state of self-hypnosis. I skeptically envisioned a large group of people, waiting, like railway passengers, waiting at the between-worlds barrier of the salon, to speak to us through Madame Clara's mouth.

Actually, I lost track of what really happened because, suddenly, I was absolutely certain that Mother was nearby. I thought I heard a man weeping as he tried to communicate with his five year old daughter, but I sat there almost as rigid as Madame, all my senses probing for the source of the familiar vibrations of criticism and disapproval that had emanated from my mother ever since I got old enough to spend money. My pumping heart was crying "Mother! Mother, where are you?" but I was suffocated by my anxiety to locate her and I made no audible sound.

I could smell, unmistakably, the odor of her homemade face cream. She used to take a mason jar and an old-fashioned rotary beater and whip up an excellent face cream out of very inexpensive ingredients. For as long as I can remember, there was always a jar of the stuff in our refrigerator. It smelled like horse chestnuts in bloom. The nostalgic fragrance made me frantic to find her and

I was about to leave the table and search the dim corners of the room, when Madame said, "Jeanette! Jeanette Heron! Someone is here to speak with Jeanette

"Yes! I cried. Oh yes, I know! Mother?"

Madame Clara's prettily tinted little mouth opened and her mesmerized voice said, "Jeanette! Are you there, Jeanette?"

My disappointment was so sudden and so sickening it was like a seizure. I sat with my elbows clamped against my ribs and squeezed my trembling chin with my hands until the worst of it had passed. Mother had never called me Jeanette in her life. I had stopped using "Jenny", which I considered a donkey's name, and had given myself the more elegant name of "Jeanette" when I got my first job. That was in Indianapolis, a long time ago, but I had always remained Jenny to my mother.

The witless voice still nagged at me: "Did you want to ask me something, Jeanette?"

"No!"

"Are you troubled?"

"No!"

"Can I help you?"

"No!"

"Then, goodbye, Jeanette. Be happy!"

That clinched it! If, through the leniency of God, or the miraculous workings of ESP, my mother had been able to give me a message, she would never have wasted it on "Be happy!" She might have said, "Take no risks," or "Work hard," or "Be frugal." Such advice, if followed, can produce measurable results, but I knew that my mother considered happiness a chancy thing, too ephemeral to have any value. If she couldn't save it until she really needed it, then she didn't want it. I ran out so quickly that the assistant had to follow me down the corridor with my coat and purse.

An ornamental tree cast a black splotch across the walk leading from Madame's apartment building to the street. I stopped in the concealing darkness to get a grip on myself, and while I stood wiping my eyes, Mother said, "Jenny!" I tried to believe that I still had a hangover from my emotional binge with the spiritualist, but I couldn't, so I called out, "Mother?"

"What is it, Jenny?" I couldn't resist looking all around me. The tinted flood lamps that spread a sickly brilliance over the lawns and brought out sparkling bits of grit in the walks also revealed clearly that there was no one within yards of me. I hadn't expected there would be.

"I wanted to ask you about the money, Mother."

"Why?" She asked, It's your money now. I have no further say about what is done with it." How well I knew that tone, a mixture of regret, resentment and dismay. I'd heard it all my life whenever anything was lost, or damaged or <u>wasted.</u>

A flood of love and understanding melted its way through me, and I said, "Mother, you lied to me and, to yourself maybe, when you said you were slaving and penny pinching for my benefit. I don't know why I believed you unless it was because you said it so many times. I laughed. Do you know what you were, Mother? A miser! A natural hoarder! You left me all that money because you had no better choice. If you could have taken it with you, I doubt if I would ever have seen a dollar of it!"

Mother laughed too. "Well, it's true I never much enjoyed spending, but I got a lot of pleasure out of saving."

Paradoxically, now that I realized the money hadn't been saved just for me, I had no compunction about taking it. "Do you have any regrets, Mother, about never going anywhere or buying yourself any nice things?"

"None whatever. I'm a little sorry about the bicycle."

"The bicycle? Oh, yes, the bicycle for my twelfth birthday. Don't give it another thought, Mother. I'm going to have a cottage with roses, and a boat, and a little new boathouse.

"I thought you might," Mother said sourly. "Still, it's not really a bad investment, but Jenny…"

"Yes, Mother?"

"Don't you ever, ever again, let me catch you throwing away hard-earned money on a silly séance!" She made a sound of disgust, then, in spiteful mimicry of Madame Clara, she intoned, "Goodby, Jeanette. Be happy!"

After You Win, What Then?

Jesus! What kind of fun-house junk do they make these hotel mirrors out of? I don't look like a man who has just come off winner in the toughest life and death game of his career. I look more like mourners hanging around the chalet, waiting for the search party to bring down the dead.

I should go out for some air and sun.

For all I know, it could be raining. "Rain falls within my sorry heart, like rain upon the town." Villon? Verlaine? Who cares? I've been in this room twelve hours and haven't even opened the drapes to look out the window. Might as well see what's out there.

The sills are filthy. The windowsills are always sooty in this town. I could just as well have gone on home without stopping here. I wasn't all that tired. There's no rain, just people walking in the yellow sunshine. From up here they look like slow insects wading through mucilage.

I ought to go out, buy a paper, maybe.

There'll be a lot of sentimental hoo-ha in the papers about finding Moya Brandt under the snow. I wonder if they'll be able to identify Pelton. He had lots of names and nationalities. The other climbers won't get much attention, but heaven help them, they're just as dead as Brandt and Pelton.

Newspaper reporter. That's what I thought the sandy haired guy was when he sat down at my table. Features a little too coarse, too dramatic. Messy, expensive clothes, like an actor playing a reporter in the movies. It was careless of me to just assume he was a reporter.

"I'm Jeff Carlysle," he said.

Voice was good. Why do I always feel inferior to people educated at eastern schools?

"Dabney," I told him, "Rufus Dabney."

I wonder how, without lifting a finger, he got the waiter to bring hot toddies. Maybe I should call down for a bottle and some ice. I guess not. I'd feel like a lush drinking alone in this lifeless room.

Carlysle wanted to know if I was a fan of Moya Brandt's. I told him no, and he said, "I hope they find her early. I don't want to wait around while they dig the others out. It could take days. There are eight of them on that mountain."

"Nine," I told him. "Pelton is up there, and that makes nine."

I always think of him as Pelton, because that was the name he had when I was first set out to get him. I wonder if he sometimes remembered who he really was.

Sharp bastard. Had me outclassed and outmaneuvered from the start. Always stayed in cities. Slipped from place to place, indistinct as a carp in a murky pool, gliding in and out among the waterweeds.

Had to take a lot of guff from some of the fellows in my section. They kidded me about Pelton paying me to lag behind. Gristle-brains! He could have paid me, all right. Must have piled up a fortune. But I couldn't get near him.

Carlysle looked miserable. I asked him if he was a friend of Miss Brandt's. I think he was keeping the mugs filled so I wouldn't wander off and leave him alone.

"No, no," he said. "Just a fan. I have copies of as many of her films as I can get. She was a goddess, a fervid, exuberant woman who generated joy the way other people generate body heat. She had a magic that could make a trip to the mailbox exciting."

"And a trip up the mountainside," I said, "an adventure to end all adventures."

I was a little drunk, but I had no right to make smart cracks to Carlysle about his dead goddess.

He looked sick.

"Who is Pelton?" he asked me.

"An assassin. A killer for hire."

Pay him enough and he'd kill anybody; an Arabian oil prince, a president, your mother. What's the difference? If he couldn't get at his victims singly, he'd bomb a plane, sink a ship, derail a train. He was a killing mechanism that homed in on the target, regardless of its location. All those helpless people! Pelton never noticed their existence.

Well, Pelton was like any other mechanism. He could be manipulated. Three years! I studied him for three years. I could have been a jealous lover the way I analyzed his habits and every move he made. I almost forgot my wife.

When the Department instructed me to turn over the chase to another man, I ignored them. Silly bastards! How could any of those flea wits know Pelton the way I did?

We're putting you on another assignment, they said. Not now they weren't. Not when I was so close. Dropped a wad tracking him at my own expense. Can't tell Ruthie about that. Pelton was a master! When they sent people to bring me back, I'd learned so much from him they never laid eyes on me.

I hunted him out of the cities and into the open. Even then, the old fox outsmarted me. He arrived at the chalet ready to climb, and I had to lose an hour buying gear and clothes. I saw the Brandt party start up the slope while I was still in the chalet shop.

I don't care if I ever see another mountain. And snow I can do without too.

Malaise! This mixture of restlessness and lethargy is a malaise that keeps me sitting here when I really want to get out of this room. It's the anonymous kind of place Pelton always lived in.

After they found the first body, I switched to coffee. I wanted a clear head if they brought Pelton down. They had walkie-talkies relayed up the mountain. Someone announced that a body had been found. Carlysle and I stood at the glass a while and watched through binoculars. Couldn't see anything but snow and a few of the search party moving around the upper slope.

I could have told them where to look. The mountain was like a big white layer cake with a broad slice cut out. Someone had poured in a slanting pile of sugar to fill up the notch. Pretty as a Christmas card. And I damn near busted a blood vessel trying to circle the pretty snowfield, unseen, so I could get up high enough and come at Pelton from the side.

Carlysle came back to our table with a pot of coffee. I told him to have the walkie-talkie man send the searchers closer to the southern cliff.

He asked, " How do you know where Moya is?"

"I saw her through the glasses," I told him, "while I was looking for Pelton. I watched her off and on all day. She was a good climber, light and strong. At the rest periods she never sat still, but moved from one person to another, like she couldn't breathe ordinary air, but needed an admixture of flattery and approval to survive. Charming, a little too deliberately charming. Too provocative." I really despised that dumb little actress.

"It wasn't admiration she was after," Carlysle said. "There was an expectancy about her, as though she assumed each hour of her life would bring a fresh and vivid experience. She had a wonderful way of making people around her feel that they too were on the verge of a wonderful life."

I'll bet she had! You could wrap my Ruthie in a bed sheet and a yashmak and she'd still have more sex appeal than that blond wiggle tail.

So why don't I go home to Ruthie? Why do I sit here reliving yesterday for the twentieth, the hundredth time?

"If you watched her, you saw it all," Carlysle said. "Tell me how it happened."

I don't know why I told him. I think it was because I could see he was a true-blue, solid-state snob and I knew he would never in God's world have sought my company except on that day and under those circumstances.

I wanted him to know I could do something he couldn't do. That there were men I could kill without penalty. Even get a commendation for it.

About mid-afternoon, I located Pelton through the glasses. And he spotted me, behind a jumble of rocks and snow. I had laid down my bow and my rifle, so I suppose he couldn't see them, but he would never make the mistake of thinking I'd come after him unarmed. He had a rifle too, but he made no effort to shoot. That puzzled me at the time because I had him cornered. He couldn't get over the mountain without coming out on the snowfield where he'd be a clear target for a man aiming from cover.

"Then I saw what he had in mind. The climbers were coming along pretty fast and he meant to join them and use them for a screen all the way up to the lodge. Maybe grab a hostage."

"Moya?" Carlysle asked.

"No, but he almost got her. During a rest stop, she scampered off, going up the slope near the base of the cliff. God knows why! Just to get attention, I imagine.

"She always moved around so much they didn't miss her right at first. Then, the guide saw her and called her name, making motions with his hands. I couldn't tell what he wanted and I don't guess she could either, because she just pulled off her cap and waved it at him. The guide went scrambling after her and those fool climbers jumped up and followed the guide."

Carlysle made a grieving sound.

"I left all my equipment except the bow and arrows and started crawling like a worm through the hell-invented snow. My bow is almost an extension of my own nervous system. I've used it to kill deer and cougar and water moccasins. I can practically thread a needle with it.

"Moya," Carlysle reminded me.

"Pelton was backed against a cliff, concealed by a rib of rock, waiting for her. When I got close enough, I stripped off the waterproof cover and strung the bow. Pelton might have got me then, but again, he didn't shoot. Maybe he was concentrating too hard on Moya Brandt. I shot him through the breast, as easy as a cardboard target."

That's just how I felt about it. I'd thought the day I got Pelton would be the greatest day of my life, but I crawled back through the snow feeling like I'd shot a cardboard target. Nothing more.

"Miss Brandt climbed on up to where Pelton had fallen and began screaming her empty head off. There was no reason for it. He could have meant no more to her than a dead deer or a sack of stones. I think she must have wanted the men in her party to come rushing to her side. When she saw the guide waving his arms like a maniac, she grabbed up Pelton's rifle and fired it three times, like in the movies, and brought ten thousand tons of snow down on them all.

I should have killed her. It might have saved the others. I had more arrows. I just didn't think of it until now.

Carlysle said, "I'm a married man. I can't even claim her body."

Poor Carlysle, who was only a fan of Moya's? Poor Carlysle, who was a liar, who had just lost the one great love of his life, and rain falls within his sorry heart. Poor Carlysle is a tycoon.

I could tell when they brought Pelton down, because the arrow shaft, unbroken by the avalanche, was standing upright between the edges of the tarp they'd wrapped him in. I'd waited all day to see him, to gloat, or something. But I couldn't look. I didn't want to see him dead. I knew then that, in the past three years, Pelton was the only thing that had given zest and substance to my life and I was as much bereft as Carlysle; my sorry heart.

Carlysle thinks I'm responsible for Moya's death. It's scum like me and Pelton, he says, who destroy innocent people with our murderous games. So, he's going to hire Pelton to kill me.

I ought to go out, but I guess I'll have dinner sent up. It may take Carlysle a while to find another Pelton, but then again, maybe he already knows one. I'd better wait for him. I'm anxious to get started.

Never Return A Gift-Horse

Blanche Stratton, cuddling a telephone between shoulder and jaw, stood in her kitchen stirring something in a saucepan on the stove. The kitchen, computerized, transistorized and sanitized, shimmered with baked enamel efficiency and ceramic elegance.

"Of course, I'll do it, Madge," she said. "I'll come over tomorrow and get the list. It's something I can do to make up for calling you in the middle of the night. You can depend on me."

"Yes, I know everybody says I'm good natured and dependable. At least I do my share of committee work, visit the sick and console the bereft. I must say, though, I'm getting weary of Adeline Cox grieving over her daughter. It's been three years since that child died and I've reached a point where sympathy is turning to annoyance. You'd think she could have come to terms with circumstance by now.

"Did I have a good time? Well of course I did. You know I'm just the kind of easygoing person who has a wonderful time wherever she is. Not that I'd have gone to Miami Beach if I hadn't followed Breck Sanders down there. The town's not the same since so many of our brethren from the islands moved in. You know perfectly well, Madge, I've never been a bigot in my life, but there's no denying that a city with a homogenous population is cleaner, safer and more progressive than one with a smorgasbord of mixed races. Some of the immigrants are very obliging, though, if you pay them enough.

"No, I never got a chance to spend much time with Breck. He was sharing a room with another conventioneer to cut down expenses. We had drinks a couple of times at a bar in the hotel.

"Yes, Madge, I know it's past your bedtime, but I wanted to ask if you've ever made Turkish delight. This stuff seems too thin. I thought it would be thicker, more like pudding. It could be too hot. I'm not sure I know how to use the stove. Mrs. Wren was already cooking for us when Sam went to sleep before I started my project. Breck never eats sweets. That's one of the ways he keeps himself so gorgeous, but he says he can't resist Turkish delight.

"Well, naturally, Madge, I could have just bought some at Sinbad's, but I wanted to do this with my own little hands.

"I hoped you wouldn't ask. To tell the truth, I came home a week ago Tuesday, but I didn't call you because I had a lot of worry on my mind and didn't want to infect anyone else.

"Well, what do you think? Who else besides Breck could make me worry? Who would have thought that dreamy-eyed, golden-haired hunk of muscle had scruples? A dollar value on how much he would accept?

"All the stuff I sent him anonymously was fairly modest, a watch, a money clip, a nice painting, things like that. But one day I got tipsy and bought him a sports car!

"I know, Madge, I know. But I paid cash for it out of my inheritance from my first husband that Sam doesn't know I have. But that fool, Breck, left the car in front of his house and is running to all the car dealers in town, trying to find out who sent it. As if he didn't know! He says he wants to give it back! I should have stayed with dumb little presents he might have bought for himself.

"No, silly, Sam isn't going to find out. I love the excitement, the, you know, the sweet obsession, the anticipation of secret meetings more than I love the man himself. In spite of his physique and his actor-ish eyes, he's not half the man Sam is. After all, Sam's worth several million.

"Hey, this stuff is getting thicker. You've no idea how hard it was to get the ingredients, here and there in several different towns between here and Florida. The main one, of course, I got from an obliging immigrant, born on some voodoo island or other.

"Now, Madge, stop teasing. We've been friends since kindergarten. I know so much about you, you'd never dare say a word. Isn't it nice? I can tell you anything! Good night, Madge."

Once There Were Two Robbers

The man in brown looked at the man in gray with a swaggering glance and, approaching the garment bag lying on the bench, dragged the zipper-tab downward to disclose the dead face of Jockey Mayo. Jockey, even with the peace of death upon him, looked neurotic and dishonest. His nose had bled a little and, in the bad light, he seemed to have an unfamiliar dark mustache. The brown man, standing so that his bulk shielded his movements, opened the bag fully and ran gloved hands over and under the light body, feeling in the dead man's pockets and into the corners of the bag as well. When his fingers found the deep depression in the back of Jockey's head, he closed the bag.

It had not yet been four o'clock, but was already thick dusk when the two men converged upon each other at the passenger stop marked "Rackham" on the railway line from the resort town to the city.

The man in brown had a compact, springy look about him, and his merry little eyes were the same bright, reddish brown as his hat, which he wore tilted to show the white hair that made his complexion so rosy by contrast.

The man in gray was dressed in speckled tweed. Although larger and younger than the man in brown, he appeared to be less lively of disposition, more ponderous and flaccid in movement.

The passenger stop was provided with a shed, built with the long side parallel to the track. The back and ends were covered by wooden siding, but there was no front wall to the structure, which was almost dark inside.

The men took positions a little way into the shed, standing a few distrustful yards apart, with shoulders hunched against the cold and hands rammed into their overcoat pockets.

The brown man's feet went "thock, thock" as he knocked one perfectly buffed shoe against the other to aid circulation in his toes. He looked at the low-hanging sky and said, "Snow, maybe."

The gray man stood motionless, ignoring his chance companion. His pale slab of a face and colorless eyes faintly expressed boredom and he gazed at the track on which, anywhere from twenty minutes to an hour behind schedule, the city bound train would eventually arrive.

The brown man said nothing more, but an atmosphere of chill hostility seemed to fill the shed, along with the gnawing mist that tortured their ankles.

The resort town of Alpine lay at the end of the line, eight miles beyond Rackham. It had been established in the days when wealthy men built modest, fifteen or twenty room cottages around the spring fed lake that gave the place its name. To these dwellings the owners sent their families, accompanied by servants, pets, friends and relatives, to spend the summer season away from the heat and tedium of the city.

When commuting became feasible and fashionable, persons of even greater wealth had bought up the fine old houses as year-round residences. Alpine, circumscribed by a wide belt of privately owned acreage belonging to country clubs, riding stables and boarding schools, had been judiciously modernized through the years, but had been enlarged hardly at all. Buffered as it was against run of the mill incomes, it remained a little, gold filled pocket, often cited as having one of the richest per capita populations in the country.

Above the heads of the men at the way station, a porcelain coated reflector spread its shallow protection over a bare light bulb. Stung to life by a timer, this antique fixture flared suddenly into brilliance, giving a jaundiced tinge to the faces of the waiting men.

The light revealed that the shelter had been painted a spinach green inside and out, and glinted on the fretwork of anti-Puritan graffiti, produced by the pocketknives and pencils of several generations of rebels. A wide shelf of painted planks, intended for use as a bench, ran around all three interior sides of the building. On one wall, an ancient dispenser with V-shaped tin pockets, empty for years, said "Take One." Somebody had left on the bench a well-filled garment bag of the kind used for storing winter coats. It looked stranded and sad in the unpleasant light.

The men, at first, were indifferent to the bag, assuming that some wayfarer had unaccountably mislaid a crucial piece of luggage, but as the minutes passed, the contours of the bag seemed to invite their speculation with greater and greater insistence.

The sprightly man in brown, wishing, perhaps, to learn whether the gray man would examine the bag, if left alone, or whether, in fact, he already knew what it contained, sauntered onto the platform, as if to look down the track. He found the footpath that marched along the crest of the embankment and followed it until he was out of sight of the other man, who watched him steadily from the shelter. Once he was lost in darkness, the brown man whirled and sprinted back to the shed.

With the coming of night, a wind had risen, knifing the mist to shreds and setting up a skeletal rattle among the denuded bushes along the embankment. Clumps of dead grass hissed with the sound of sand being scattered endlessly onto a sheet of paper.

The man on the footpath had counted on these noises to camouflage his movements, but the man in gray must have heard something, for he was standing exactly as before when his fellow traveler reached the shed. Inside, however, there was a feeling that something had just happened, as though the frosty air still held the imprint of recent activity.

The man in brown glanced at the bag and saw that the pull-tab, which had been snugged into its lock, was now flipped up at an angle, two inches below its proper closure. That was how he came, at length, to find Jockey Mayo, bagged like a turkey, with the back of his head caved in.

The man in brown laid a consoling hand on the garment bag, then returned to his former place. Although it was now plain that they had become adversaries, he might have tried, yet again, to squeeze an informative comment from his unspeaking companion, but two young men in sheep-lined jackets came quietly in out of the darkness.

One of them was bareheaded, relying on earmuffs and his bushy tan beard for warmth. The other wore a watch cap over black hair, which hung in a stringy fringe to his shoulders. He had unfolded the high collar of his sweater and drawn it over his undefended chin. For a moment, they muttered together in secretive exchange, then one of them said, with slight overemphasis, "Let's go up to the filling station. We can get a ride there."

The other one asked, "How long do you think it will take to get a lift?"

There was another murmured conference, then the dark young man answered clearly, "Not more than thirty or forty minutes."

"Then we'd better move it, man!" his friend urged. "Let's move it!" As quietly as they had come, they left the shed.

"Odd thing!" the brown man said, "Those young fellows couldn't see you. They looked me over close enough, but never once looked at you!" He gestured toward the bag that contained Jockey Mayo's remains. "Couldn't see that either. You might say they were downright diligent about not seeing it."

The gray man made his first speech of the evening. "What's it to you?" he asked distantly, but his light eyes reflected a wary uneasiness, as if he realized, too late, that he had fallen in with a madman.

Then, as though it were now his turn to play the leader in some weird game, the man in gray wandered to the edge of the platform, as the brown man had done earlier, and loped heavily down the footpath.

The other man was after him in a flash, following within touching distance.

"What do you think you're doing?" the gray man yelled, turning back with arms and legs outspread, barring his pursuer's advance.

"Why, I'm going wherever you go," the man in brown assured him. "I heard you set it up with those young guys to meet at a filling station. They said they'd have a car."

Before the man in gray could defend himself, the brown man had been over him in a brisk search, patting pockets, ribs and waistband.

"What are you looking for?"

"I don't know. Something as big as a briefcase or as small as a key."

From far down the track they heard the blare of a whistle. And the man in gray eased his straddling stance. The man in brown may have suspected that his opponent meant to knock him under a train. Certainly, he could see that the gray-gloved fist could strike like a mallet, if its owner were allowed enough time. He skipped nimbly out of reach.

The evening Express to Alpine sped past, snickering lightly as it tried to outrun the sound of its own whistle. The men had a glimpse, brief and blurred, of card players in the club car, diners lingering at white covered tables and passengers seated in warm, lighted coaches. Then they were alone again with their enmity.

"Listen!" the brown man commanded.

From Rackham came the voices of neighbor talking to neighbor, unusual on such a wintry night. Lights spread across the backyards that crowded up against the right-of-way and a chimney pulsed luridly as the revolving light of a police car swept over it.

Two police officers, with powerful flashlights, came down the between-yards sidewalk that gave public access to the station. They circled the shed, going in and out of it, then separated and walked away from each other along the embankment, swinging their torches.

"They won't search the shelter again," the gray man suggested.

At the policeman's ominous approach, the two travelers, at a truce for the moment, moved softly away from the footpath and took a diagonal course toward the station, squatting in the thin shadow of leafless growth, whenever the beam came their way. When they got back to the shed, the bag was gone.

"Round one goes to you!" the brown man said, his handsome teeth exposed in a tigerish smile. "I missed the 'move it' cue, didn't I? Your boys took the bag before the cops got here. Where were they going with it?"

The man in gray chose not to answer. He was looking at the blazing, white eye of the approaching city-bound train.

This train was not the sleek princess of the express runs. The one-coach train that pulled up at the platform was more like a tiresome old nanny, loved and detested by all who depended on her as she trundled up and down, taking care of everyone in her exasperating way.

The man in gray hung back, neither boarding the train, nor leaving the platform, but waiting stolidly, as if hoping his brown clad tormentor would leave without him. As they waited, three young girls in party clothes, a couple of housemaids and a man with a guitar came down from Rackham and took their places in the train. When the platform was empty, the man in gray still lingered, closely attended by the man in brown.

Up on the embankment, a windswept policeman tapped his leg with his still burning flashlight, while he talked with the engineer. In gusty fragments, they heard him say something about a dead man on the track.

Suddenly, the gray man lunged into the coach, with the brown man, quick and agile, behind him, pressing him forward so that he was obliged to either take a seat selected by his shepherd, or start a brawl on the train. At the front end of the vintage car they found double seats opposite each other. They dropped into these, face-to-face, their knees almost touching.

As the train started with a weak, forward surge, the two young men in sheepskin jackets jumped lightly down from the roof of the shed and boarded the moving train. Without seeming to notice the two men sitting so cozily together, they took places directly across the aisle. The tan beard of the larger young man did not quite conceal the garment bag, folded and stuffed under his jacket.

The brown man leaned forward, his little eyes glinting like nail heads. "The fellow in the bag was my friend Jockey Mayo. We went up to Alpine today to rob a bank."

The man in gray became as still as stone. "What time?" he asked.

"As close to two-thirty as makes no difference."

The gray man shot a glance at the two young men across the aisle, then, as if to retract the involuntary movement, turned and looked at his reflection in the dark window.

The brown man smiled his ferocious smile. You sent them into the bank about the same time, didn't you?"

The gray man considered his answer thoroughly.

The conductor called, "Granville, Granville" as he moved from seat to seat, clicking his ticket-punch and selling tickets to passengers who had boarded without them.

"They went in a little later than that," the man in gray finally admitted. "It looks like you and Mayo blew it."

"Probably," said the man in brown, "though I've never known Jockey to fail."

"I don't suppose riding this rattletrap is part of your original plan."

"No," said the man in brown. "We had a van this morning. Took it from behind one of those thrift shops run for charity. It wasn't a good car, but Jockey wanted it, because it had a sign on the side that said, 'Happiness is Sharing.' Jockey was light hearted. I'm going to miss him."

The two men leaned toward each other, intently playing a game in which each ventured large scraps of unimportant information in the hope of gaining the tiny, crucial piece that mattered. The brown man played first.

"We drove to Alpine and stopped in the parking lot, right near the back door. The door's a heavy, metal job with no lock or handle on the outside.

"I'd done a little research before-hand so when we spotted a white caddy in the lot, I went into the bank and told one of the girls I'd just dented a white Cadillac and would wait outside by the door that opens into the parking lot. The bank manager drives a white Caddy. He came out right away."

"Pretty risky," the man in gray said. "He might have done ten other things besides come out."

"Disappointing, maybe, but not risky. We gave him ninety seconds. If he hadn't come, we would have driven away. There are lots of other banks. But he did come out. Jockey grabbed the door and held it open, while I tranquilized the manager with a jolt on the chin. I backed him into the bank and waltzed him through a door marked 'Conference Room'. I left him there, taped and tied, in the coat closet."

"If you'd waited a few more minutes," the gray man said, with an odd quirk to his mouth, "the bank guard would have opened the door for you. He was in with us for a percentage. It was dumb to try that job with just two men."

"That's why Jockey wanted to go through the parking lot door. You know that bank. They've kept it just like it was in 1890, with the tellers working behind a wall of marble and gilded wrought iron. The best way to get to them is through the back. And Jockey meant to get help from the guard by grabbing one of the women and threatening to blow her head off."

"We had pretty much the same routine laid out," the gray man said. "We were going to make a show of whacking the guard over the head when we left, so he could lie down and look innocent." His lips stirred in what could have been a smile. "He would have helped Mayo, all right, thinking he was one of my boys. He had never seen any of us, except me. Do you think Mayo got away with a bundle?"

"Maybe. I never saw him again, alive."

Engrossed in their game, the men had become too tense to hear the conductor and were surprised when the train stopped. The gray man dragged a hand through the steam on the window and, looking through the cleared streak, said, "Widow's Landing." Two teenage boys in parkas came in.

"Odd thing!" the man in brown commented. "After I dumped the manager, I went out the back door to keep an eye on things. Jockey had brought along a thick roll of newspapers and jammed them in the door to keep it from closing. I left them there and went around front and looked in. Everybody was going about their business, calm as you please. There were two customers in the bank and the guard was standing just behind the glass at the front door, looking at his watch."

The brown man sat reviewing his bafflement for a moment. "Odd thing!" he repeated. "I wonder where Jockey was."

"So." The gray man prodded.

"So, I circled the bank and came back to the lot." An expression of sinister merriment brightened his face. "I guess that's when you sent your boys in, while I was on the other side of the bank."

The gray man shrugged indifferently, but excitement tinged his cheekbones the faintest pink.

"You said Mayo never showed?"

"That's right. He wasn't much overdue, but I was sure something had curdled. I didn't like sitting in the van, unless someone came looking for the manager and recognized me as the Caddy smasher who had been in the bank. I moved back among the parked cars and that was a bad move. I couldn't find a spot where I could see the door, the van and the front corner of the bank all at the same time."

"I told you, you needed more people."

"I was about to go back to the van," the brown man continued, "when I heard sirens and, before I could get out from between the cars, the van was gone. I assumed it was Jockey. I looked around for a car and found somebody's Peugeot with the motor running and drove it to the railway station. Police cars were swarming before I'd gone a block and it didn't seem like the best day for driving a stolen automobile out of town."

A delicate spasm of emotion that might have been outrage moved the gray man's impassive face. "That was mine!" he said. "You took my car!"

"Tell me about it," the brown man invited.

The passenger with the guitar began gently playing "Greensleeves"

The gray man said, "We cruised past the bank soon after two-thirty. Everything was as peaceful as Sunday. I let the boys out near the rear entrance. Then I backed out of the lot and took a space at the curb and waited with the motor running. I was too busy to see the boys go inside, but, when I looked, they were gone, so I figured the guard was on his toes. I'd been waiting about two minutes when I heard the sirens,"

The brown man laughed. "That must have jarred you! Sending your little scavengers in just in time to meet the fuzz!"

The gray man gazed at the man in brown with pallid malevolence.

"No way," he said. "There was no way the cops could be on to us so soon. I went up front to see what was happening and there were cops all over the bank and more searching the parking lot...I got caught in the crowd gawking at the bank and the police made us move along. When I finally got back to my car, it was gone. At the time, I thought the boys had taken it. I didn't see them again until they came into the Rackham station."

"Is that all you've got?" the brown man asked.

"That's all. How did you get out of Alpine?"

"While I was at the Alpine station, I looked up a Rackham address in the phone book and took a cab. Miscalculated a little and had to walk a quarter of a mile to the train stop. You?" Again, a tiny tremor of emotion disturbed the gray man's face. "I walked all the way from the bank to the Alpine station and found out there wasn't another train for more than an hour. I went to the freight depot out behind the station and saw a kid loading cartons onto a pickup. For five bucks, he drove me to Rackham.

The unnerving expression of merriment had come back into the brown man's eyes. He sat forward confidentially, his clasped hands hanging between his spread knees, and said, "When you put it all together, we don't, either one, have a thing. Call your boys over!"

The man glanced across the aisle at the figures in sheepskins. The younger men stared back with a look that was at once sulky and placating.

All the passengers were gone, except for a young couple dozing against each other. When it was empty, the coach appeared to be dingier, the light dimmer and it seemed to be late at night, although it was barely dinnertime.

"What do you want?" the gray man asked.

"I want to know what happened to Jockey and the money. He got it all right. He never missed."

"Why should we tell you anything?"

The brown man smiled. "Because this is just a little, bitty gun, but it can pulverize your kneecap."

The gray man examined his companion's loosely cupped hands and saw the short barrel of a tiny gun peeping evilly at him from under its' owner's thumb. He crooked a finger at the two across the aisle and they came over, sliding reluctantly into the spare seats.

The gray man said, "Roy and Bernie. Roy is the black haired one. Bernie has the beard. Boys, tell us about the fellow in the bag."

The young men sat silent, making small gestures of protest, until, under the heartless, pale gaze of the man in gray, they grew as calm as doomed mice.

"We saw you moving the car," the black-haired Roy said.

"There was no one anywhere around and then, all of a sudden, there was this little scoutmaster type, wearing lederhosen and knee socks, standing between us and the door. Just came out of nowhere."

"Would you believe, the bank?" the brown man asked.

"He couldn't have!" Bernie denied through his beard. "We never took our eyes off the door."

"Get on with it," the gray man said, rubbing his knee as if it ached.

"The little guy looked funny," Roy continued, "like maybe he knew us. He started to run. I grabbed him, but I couldn't have held him, except Bernie cracked him behind the ear with that bag of buckshot he carries around."

"I didn't mean to hurt him," Bernie said. "I only wanted to stop him running to the cops."

The man in brown murmured to the man in gray, "The guard could have said something that tipped him to your operation."

"We caught him under the arms," Roy went on, "and dragged him into the bank between us. The guard had fixed the door, like he said he would."

The train stopped at Hag's Hill and the thieves fell silent as fifteen or twenty hard-hatted workmen with lunch boxes came into the train. There was snow on their shoulders.

The train moved again and, above the hubbub of masculine voices, the brown man said to Roy, "Go on."

"About three yards inside the door," Roy said, "The guard was kneeling over a woman on the floor. He had a bleeding knot on the side of his head and was trying to peel a strip of tape off her mouth. When he saw me and the scoutmaster and Bernie, he went spastic and started screaming, 'Get out of here! You've already robbed us once! You didn't say you were coming back! I've turned in the alarm! I've turned in the alarm!'

"Bernie dropped his half of the scoutmaster and ran. I grabbed the little guy in both arms and that's when I knew he was dead. I lugged him with me to the parking lot. I didn't want to get the police all excited over a dead body."

Bernie turned to the gray man like a bearded child with a grievance. "You should have stayed in the lot! If we hadn't found that van idling right outside, we'd have been busted for sure. Roy told me the dude was dead and we heard the sirens just as we pitched him into the van. I chewed Roy out for dragging him along." Bernie grinned. "But Roy said there was nothing wrong with stepping into the bank to tell the folks their back door was open. We'd be in the clear, if we could just unload Leather-britches."

Roy inclined his head toward the man in gray. "He always does the driving, so we didn't know our way around too well. We wanted to go out to this lake, but you can't get near it, unless you own a piece of the shore or have a boat. Besides it was still too light. We wound up in Rackham by accident. Then we saw this sign, like an arrow, that said 'To Station'. There were a few police cars moving around, but we stopped right on the street. There was nothing else to do. We climbed into the van and Bernie struck matches while I looked through the stuff. It was mostly old clothes and dishes. I found the bag and pulled out the coats. We zipped the little guy up in it and walked down to the station. Bernie carried the bag over his shoulder, like a piece of luggage. It was spooky!"

"That was an odd thing," the brown man said, "to leave it on the bench like that."

"It was just temporary," Bernie answered. "We went along the embankment looking for a better place to dump it, once it got really dark. We found a place, but when we came back, you guys were there."

"And your boss here went running down the embankment and got me out of the shed for you," the brown man said, as if enjoying the mischief of small boys. "Why did you come back afterwards?"

"The place we found for the scoutmaster was a dirt slide." Roy said, "Where it would be easy to have an accident. We shoved him down. He was getting a little stiff. Then, when we got back to the van, cops were fooling around it, shining their lights on the license plate. We went back to the station and climbed on the roof."

"It was growing chilly in the train and the homing workmen were quiet. The man in gray was watchful and still.

"Busy, busy, busy!" the brown man said, "but no one saw any money."

Bernie screwed up his eyes in an opinionated squint. "If you ask me," he said, "there wasn't any. Maybe the guard was up to something. When we went in, I could see into one of those little golden cages. Two girls were in there, talking and smiling. They hadn't been robbed!"

"Was …ah…the scoutmaster carrying anything?" the brown man asked.

"Nah," Roy said. "He didn't have anything but a backpack. When Bernie ran out on me, I shucked him out of it and left it in the bank. Weighed a ton."

Anguished comprehension hollowed his frantic eyes and blanched his stricken cheeks.

"He robbed the bank!" Roy breathed. "He must have stumbled over a tub full of money! Maybe he found the vault open!" He looked around at the three men watching him and said again, "It weighed a ton!"

The man in brown stood up. He showed the two young men the little gun in his hand, but it was hardly necessary. They had already pulled in their feet to make room for his passage. He tapped the garment bag showing between Bernie's coat collar and beard. "Keep holding that," he said, moving to the exit door.

The train pulled up at a deserted way-station. The snowflakes seemed to darken as they swirled past its single lamp.

"Where did you leave my car?" the gray man called.

The brown man glanced over his shoulder in wicked amusement, but did not answer. He stepped out onto the lonely platform.

"Solitaire!" the conductor announced.

Bugeeshi

On a steaming night in the mid-nineteen-twenties, when the Belgian Congo still offered much opportunity for exploitation, Georgette Prideaux roosted on the lamp suspended from the ceiling of their company bungalow and watched her husband, Paul, introduce an unwanted guest to a roomful of hastily invited friends. Because Paul was so excessively talkative, Georgette knew he was irritated and apprehensive.

"This is Norbert Mariman," Paul was saying to the two French engineers and their wives. "It's a pleasant surprise for us to have another Company Director visit us so soon, isn't it?"

He turned to Mariman, a man with pallid eyes and the face of a sunburned shark. "We had not expected BeCeKa to send anyone out from Antwerp again until after the rainy season. Meet Doctor Hilliard, our only American and our only bachelor. He's been in the Congo for years, but this is his first job with a diamond mining outfit. He says we're all unhealthy."

The Director does not find my husband exactly impressive, thought Georgette, as she watched several Bugeeshi filter through the screen door from the outside darkness. I think Paul needs me. She was ready to abandon her lamp and ease back into her body, when she saw herself draw Mariman away from Paul and motion coaxingly toward a settee. "When were you last in Paris? Sit here and tell me about Paris!" The wicker settee crackled as they took their seats and, picking up fans, they created a tiny turbulence that did, in fact, give some relief from the heat.

"Drinks are on the way," said Paul, not so nervous now, as he poured whisky into water glasses. "We may not get any ice. Our only source is the kerosene-operated refrigerator in the infirmary. And we can get ice only if the poor sick people don't need it all."

Georgette risked a quick glance at the Bugeeshi. Quite a number of them had gotten in, but they shrunk themselves to gnat size and were swimming lazily in the thick air around the other ceiling lamp. She edged around her own lamp to get a better view of herself and Mariman. I am very, very pretty in my persimmon gown, she thought. My arms are really beautiful. I doubt if anyone has mentioned how exciting a woman's arms can be since Flaubert wrote Madame Bovary.

She noticed that Doctor Hilliard was eyeing her visible self sharply. She had told him about occasionally leaving her body, and he had said, "It's the quinine. Living in the Congo is too hard on Nordic women. The quinine jiggers their menstrual cycles, and the climate, the monotony and the isolation work with the quinine to destroy their nerves. Mild hallucination is not unusual." Then on a more personal and genuinely compassionate note, he had continued, "I wish you convent-educated girls wouldn't join in the Saturday night wife-swapping games. When you shatter a value system that has been built into you since childhood, you erase the essential structure of the only self that you can recognize. You then become a pseudo-personality that you don't understand."

She knew he was absolutely right, but she knew, also, that she was trapped, like a fly under a bell jar, within the social mores of their tiny, closed community. She had smiled and shrugged, "But, Doctor, the tedium! The ennui! How else can we know it's Saturday night?"

The doctor was mistaken, of course, about hallucinations. It was the Bugeeshi. She had learned the exhilarating art of stepping outside her body from them. Vrouw Kronfeldt, a Dutch girl, incongruously named Kathleen, had warned her against going near the special trees where the Bugeeshi lived. "I have been here almost five years," she had said, "and I've never yet seen a native pass under one of these trees. If there's trouble in the village, the people might believe it's because we have annoyed the Bugeeshi, so we think it wise to observe all local injunctions against disturbing them. They are supposed to be very powerful and capricious."

Georgette was certain that she could feel the force of the invisible spirits that brooded in the lofty foliage. "Where do they come from?" she asked. "Are they holy souls? Ghosts of the dead?"

"If the natives know, they won't say," Kathleen answered. "I believe the village people think of them as demons. They neither worship them, nor ask any favors of them. The native attitude toward the Bugeeshi is mainly placatory. Thank God, they don't really exist."

In her cringing heart Georgette knew that they did exist. She took to watching the trees through binoculars and, after a while, found that she could actually see the Bugeeshi. They were sometimes tiny, sometimes gigantic, but always amorphous, alien and grotesque. They had an unwholesome fascination for her, as some loathsome thing occasionally fascinates the very fastidious. Later, the Bugeeshi began leaving their trees at intervals and coming to the bungalow. She had been certain, from the very first, that their fearful companionship was inevitable.

Now as she looked at Paul, she thought he seemed tired and troubled. His job of grading the entire output of the mine was just too exhausting. Mariman was saying, "As the natives grow more sophisticated, the rate of theft rises. We've installed fluoroscopes at the southern mines to catch the fellows who swallow a diamond now and again. We're tightening up all our operations. At this site, we plan to station armed Belgian guards at points where theft is most feasible. This will mean, regrettably, that most of you, as well as the native laborers, will work under constant observation. In the future, the ladies will leave the compound only on designated days, when guards are available to accompany them."

In the dumbfounded silence following Mariman's pronouncement, Georgette heard herself say in a mechanical voice that seemed to lack volition, "No! Really, I can't stay here any longer. If I don't see shops and theaters and snow and a real church soon, I shall perish. I've been begging Paul to take me home!"

Mariman smiled his shark's smile, "He signed a five-year contract, Mme. Prideaux. Have you read the forfeiture clause? If your husband breaks his contract, he will owe BeCeKa more than he can earn in France in two years. You can always go back to Paris alone, of course."

"I shall never do that," the toneless voice said. "I have no inclination to become a make-believe widow for nearly three years. Paul must come with me. Prison would be better than this place."

From her perch on the lamp, Georgette saw that the Bugeeshi had spread themselves into thin veils that swirled in slow eddies above the coffee table. She saw, too, that Paul was surreptitiously and frantically patting his wife's wrist. That poor little thing is making a deplorable mess of herself, Georgette thought. I must go down and help her. She found that she could not move. One of the Bugeeshi, with enormous, distorted eyes, welded her with his gaze to the fluted reflector of her lamp. While she strained wildly against it and screamed silently, she saw

Mariman smile even more wildly. The man seemed to have teeth from earlobe to earlobe, "We have no wish to manage a prison," he said. "Only a small, pilfer-proof mining operation."

"A hopeless wish, M'sieu Mariman!" The girl in the flame colored dress sounded like a fever patient who could control the speech of delirium. "You create your own thieves! Have you never read the childhood stories of heroes stealing jewels from dragons, giants and ogres? Diamonds are only ugly little rocks that became valuable because a cartel like BeCeKa squats down on a whole mountain of them and dares the world to touch a single pebble."

Shut up! Shut up! Shut up! whispered Georgette. She saw the girl pull away from her husband's arm. avoid the doctor's draining gesture, and move behind the bar where she scrabbled among the bottles of bitters, olives and grenadine. She brought out a rattling pint jar labeled "Pickled Pearl Onions" and waved it at Mariman. "Even Paul!" she said. "Even Paul, who despises diamonds and is the soul of honesty, has been stealing stones for the past two years!"

She allowed the jar to smash on the wooden floor, then, crying aloud like a child, she turned to her white-faced husband and wailed, "I want to go home, Paul!"

When they had all gone away, or been taken away, Georgette stretched in relief at being freed from the lamp, at last. She was very pretty, she thought, remembering the girl in the persimmon dress, but pathetic. I wonder what will happen to the poor dear now. Perhaps it's just as well that I couldn't get back in. She floated down to join her fellows as they streamed homeward toward their trees. At least, she thought, as she drifted through the humid jungle, I know now where the Bugeeshi come from.

Animal Shelter

Bethene had a fervid soul. She would sometimes walk out in the rain and laugh or yell at the sky while water drops pounded her face. For her, each day brought its own beauty with it and she enjoyed every one of them as it passed.

She sang to her spindly houseplants until they took heart and flourished. She adopted children by mail and at any given time was supporting six or eight kids in different parts of the world on the monthly installment plan, even though she sometimes had to wait tables or take in home typing to meet her obligations.

She had no interest in movements or causes. For example, she never gave a dime to the Humane Society, but took stray pets into her home, fed them, cured their ailments, washed them and cared for them until she could find placements for them with suitable families. For the hopelessly damaged, she had an arrangement with a squeamish veterinarian whereby he charged her for putting them to sleep, but he always gave the money to an animal care center.

She found the man she married lying on the beach early one morning; he'd been hideously beaten by the thugs in his own drug-running, house-breaking, horse-doping clan. One of his legs was broken and he never fully recovered the sight in one eye. He was a liar, a thief, possibly a murderer, and a little too stupid for the sharks he swam with. But Bethene loved him and, oddly, he truly loved her.

The tough boys caught him chiseling again and Bethene, to save him from the undiluted agony of their vengeance, took his gun from under his pillow and put him to sleep while they were kicking down the door.

Wine of the Country

Early one morning, the five thieves flitted out of the jungle and sidled ominously into the hut of Konok, the woodcarver. Konok was twenty, but had no wife, as he was a candidate for priesthood and would be married on the day he was formally admitted into the service of the god, Yok.

His training, begun in boyhood, had been long and rigorous, but Konok had admirably completed all prescribed duties, except the final one, which, to Konok, seemed the most difficult of all. Because the rite traditionally required the presence of at least one visitor and because Konok's backward village was not much favored by travelers, he had been able, for some time, to shirk the ultimate duty that would elevate him to the elite brotherhood.

Now, circumstance had presented him with a splendid gift of five wayfarers who might be expected to attend the celebration, but Konok longed to send the intruders back into the jungle and defer yet a while his rise to ecclesiastical eminence.

They were vicious looking men with the imprint of their evil lives upon them and they addressed each other by short, brutal names, which meant "Strangler", "Dagger", "Bonebreaker" and "Rat". Their leader, the oldest and smallest of the lot, was called "Pryd", which had no meaning that Konok could recall.

"We have come for food," they said, bowing their heads in a mockery of courtesy.

"I have a pot of peas sitting warm in the ashes," said Konok, "and sufficiency of meal-cakes and milk."

"Slop!" said the one called Bonebreaker and he gave Konok such a buffet on the jaw that his teeth were jarred in their sockets.

"Is it true," asked Rat, "that strangers asking for food at the village are always given a feast? We've had some hungry days and could well do with a banquet."

"Not always," Konok answered. "Sometimes travelers are content with less."

The man called Strangler lunged at Konok with outstretched fingers, but Pryd, looking very old and mean, raised a hand and stopped him.

Let us talk with the lad a moment," he said. Then, turning to Konok, he asked, "How do strangers obtain a feast?

"The head priest must be asked by Yok's Messenger," Konok explained. "Three years ago Grispok was Messenger."

Dagger, with his hand in his girdle, jostled Pryd, saying, "You blatting old goat! Must we wait starving while you yammer with this bumpkin about bygone times?"

Rat, too, slipped his hand into his girdle and, giving his leader a braggart's stare, went to stand beside Dagger.

"Who is the Messenger this year?" Pryd asked.

"I am," Konok answered. His eyes glistened, dark as apricot seeds, and tears crept down his boyish cheeks.

"Can you not be satisfied with cakes and milk? And the peas?"

"Milk!" cried Bonebreaker, making a spitting sound. "We want meat and wine! I could drink a tubful of wine! Pryd, send this pretty little cry-baby to the head priest!" He held his huge, clenched fists close to Pryd's eyes, then went to join Rat and Dagger.

Then Strangler said, "This fool does not pay for the feast. What can he gain by hoarding food that costs him nothing?"

And to Konok, Pryd said, "What do you gain?"

"If I go to the head priest on your behalf," Konok answered, "he will expect me to do a thing I am most unwilling to do. But I cannot refuse him. Please! Eat what is here and go away!"

Pryd looked all about the hut with his wild old lizard's eyes and said, "Milk is nourishing and peas are tasty. What matters one meal in a lifetime?"

Scowling, Strangler also jostled Pryd and, drawing a thin length of pliant leather from his sleeve, he dangled it before Pryd's face as he went to stand with his three companions.

"What will the head priest require of you?" Pryd asked Konok.

"He will insist that I become a priest."

"Why can you not refuse him?"

"Because I love his youngest daughter and only priests may wed the daughters of priests."

"I think, nevertheless, that you must go and ask him," Pryd said. "I will go with you."

"And I will go with the two of you," said Dagger, and he followed them, never taking his hand from the blade in his sash.

They went along the jungle's edge without speaking, following a dusty path that wormed its way blindly through thickets that had sprung up on once cleared land. The head priest's house, ornamented with symbols painted in black, red and yellow, lay in a great clearing spread with raked, white sand. Nothing larger than a fly could approach the house without being seen. They went in through a door of dried leather.

The room they entered was large and dim with a polished floor and colored walls. Four guards were posted about these walls with weapons in their hands. In the center of the room sat an enormous box. Its frame was made of lavishly carved wood, its sides were sheer screens of woven hair. The form of the priest reclining within the box was obscure, except for the movements of a fan that made a flickering red shadow inside the little chamber.

Konok knelt with knees, elbows, flattened palms and forehead on the polished floor. "Know, Brother of Yok, that I am

Konok, titular messenger of the god." Sighing heavily, he added, "Know also that I am a suppliant for a place among the Brothers of Yok." He waited a moment, but when the head priest made no comment he continued. "We have among us five strangers who beseech the solace of food and the benediction of wine. What answer shall I give them?"

The fan ceased its red dance, then the priest's voice, rich as music, said, "The God is pleased to offer the travelers the comfort they require. Let them rest in your house, Messenger. Before midday they shall partake of the bounty of Yok."

In a surprisingly short time after the three couriers had returned to Konok's hut, the townspeople came with trays and platters and bowls and baskets. Meats, boiled, baked and stuffed, were set before the thieves, and eggs, crammed with a savory filling. They were offered pastry and fruits and cool melons as well. A jar of wine, half as high as a man, was dragged in on a wooden sled, but was not broached until the head priest, himself, could arrive to break the seal and ladle out the first potion.

"This wine is more than wine," he told the guests. "It is a blessing from our god. To drink it is to be on a par with Yok and know the ecstasy of being divine."

The thieves swigged the heavenly vintage from great wooden goblets, to the delight of their misused palates. But they ate and drank without Pryd. He called them treacherous dogs and refused to share food with them. He found Konok's tools and sat carving a little wooden whistle to pass the time.

Speeches, flattering to the visitors, were given by the dignitaries of the place, but the thieves would not spare a moment to make polite reply. They gorged themselves, now and again making derisive remarks about the pot of peas, which still sat among the cold ashes.

Outside, children threw flowers until the house was half buried in blossoms. Accompanied by musicians, the populace marched around the dwelling, singing hymns of praise and thanksgiving to Yok.

When the diners were besotted on the glorious wine and fed almost to suffocation, torches were lighted and the table removed to make room for a procession of priests who came in with gifts. Foremost among them was Konok. He had been stripped naked and powdered with gold. Over his hair was a fluttering cap of rooster feathers. The head priest, himself, gave Konok a sharp little knife of quartz and called him Brother. A mat covered with painted symbols was laid down and Konok was sent to stand upon it while the happy thieves were adorned with wreaths of honeysuckle, heavy chains of gold, strings of cloves, bracelets of silver and girdles of woven straw, decorated with turquoises. Great anklets of brass, with knobs of garnet, were clasped around their unwashed legs.

A group of women sitting on folded legs at one end of the room began a soft lament and the head priest's daughter, Tender Squash, was led to Konok. She, too, had been stripped and sprinkled with gold. Over one arm, she carried a worked napkin of heavy cloth. In her hands she bore a little basin of scented water. Her ankles were attached to each other by a short lanyard of braided straw that could be severed readily by the quartz knife.

Gravely, Tender Squash knelt on the painted mat and placed the basin on the floor between herself and Konok. She took the napkin in both hands and continued to kneel while Konok stood before her, transfixed. Urgent drums nagged and tambourines scolded. Still, he stood, staring with glazed eyes at his lovely bride.

Uproar broke out among the thieves, who cursed and yelled in boozy outrage when they discovered that the attendant priests had insidiously linked the necklaces and bracelets and girdles and anklets to ringbolts in walls and seats, so that the guests were held captive and helpless on their benches.

The drums raged, the flutes screamed and Konok moved at last. Gritting his teeth and slinging tears from his eyes, he took the little knife and cut the visitor's throats for the greater glory of Yok.

While Konok rinsed his shaking hands in the basin and his young wife dried them on the napkin, Pryd played the hymn of thanksgiving badly, but fervently, on his new made wooden whistle.

Joint Tenancy

When the soul of Feldon Whitley had been two days in the after-life, he found the atmosphere not to his liking and went back to his body. He looked at face and figure and found neither prepossessing, but felt, nonetheless, a special regard for this soft and unreliable vehicle, which the embalmers had rendered durable, but useless.

He lingered on a riverbank, cogitating, and concluded that the best way to obtain substitute housing was to search for a soul just leaving its earthly shell and dart like a hermit crab into the vacated cavity. A suicide would do, if the carcass were not too badly damaged by the means of effecting the soul's egress.

As he pondered, a young man of twenty or so jumped from the overhead bridge into the river with a mighty splash. His hands were clasped behind his back and he made no effort to save himself. A huge, silvery bell of air rose through the tons of water closing over him.

Instantly, Whitley's soul shot down the column of bubbles issuing from the body he coveted and he found that he moved into it a moment before the resident spirit had moved out.

He twined himself around the departing soul and, against his own best interests, entreated: "Don't do it! It's awful afterwards. I just came from there."

"Mind your own business," said the imprisoned soul. "Whatever it is. It will surcease from what I am suffering."

"It's all dim nothing!" Whitley's soul cried. "No light, no color, no sound, not another soul to be seen. At least not in the district I was in. Might have been Limbo."

"That's what I'm after!" said the writhing soul. I gave my love, my life, my every wish and thought to the adoration of a woman who could not love me in return. Limbo can't be as desolate as my earthly existence."

"That's not love, you fool. That's obsession! Hang on now! I hear a motorboat."

The captive soul gave a convulsive twist and was gone. Whitley's soul tried to urge the precious body upward and was assisted by strong hands and a hook. Once they had it in the boat, they squeezed the water out of it and turned it over, face up. "My

God!" said one of the men in the boat, "This is the guy they've been looking for. Talk about luck!"

By the time the two detectives came, the body was in fair shape and Whitley's soul was almost at home in it. The men took it to a room in a high building, where they asked many questions, beginning with, "Why did you kill her, Lang?"

Whitley's soul explained to them that Lang's soul, all that was essentially Lang, had been expelled in the river and was gone, most likely forever. "This," he said, "is only the resuscitated body, which is now mine by squatter's right. I know nothing of any killing. I know only that the man's soul deserted him because of hopeless love."

They made him repeat his story many times. They gave him a lie detector test. They changed their tactics and pretended to believe him. They stopped calling him Lang.

"What's your name?" they asked.

"I don't know. You lose your name in Limbo."

"What do you do for a living?"

"I don't know, but in my soul, I feel that I am an artist. Probably a painter or sculptor."

"She was a model! Why did you kill her?"

"Who? Kill who?"

The man at the desk made a phone call and waited, playing silent piano scales with one hand. When he hung up, he said, "Feldon Whitley, fifty-seven, an artist, was killed day before yesterday when he fell from a ladder while hanging a large painting in his studio."

The men talked together and the one at the desk made another phone call. A man with five pens in his top jacket pocket came in and listened to a tape recording of the interrogation, then chatted awhile with Whitley's soul. To the two men, he said, "I think we can risk it. It's very interesting. I'd like to go with you."

Lang's body and Whitley's soul, accompanied this time by three men, went to a mortuary. They entered by a side door and went to a place where a casket was waiting to be wheeled into the chapel. An attendant opened the coffin and waited nearby.

"Do you remember her?" asked the man with the pens.

Whitley's soul looked at the glittering filaments of golden hair piled prodigally over the little satin pillow, the fragile temples, the brows that were winged poems, the lashes of dark silk that painted the cold cheeks with mystery. He gazed at the heart-wrenching mouth, just ready to smile, tinted a pale rose color, at the proud rondure of the breasts under cream silk and at the pale hands that were marvels of articulated grace.

"God in heaven!" he said. "If she looks like this now, think what she must have been when she could laugh and walk and blow kisses. Who could destroy a beauty like this?"

"You could, bastard!" said one of the detectives. "You took a club and…'

"Don't tell me how she died! I don't want her disfigured in my mind. What color were her eyes?"

None of them could answer, except the attendant, who came forward softly. "Dark," he said, "but not brown or blue, a mixture of both. Gray. Like moleskin."

The three men urged Whitley/Lang away and, later, they put him in a cell. He hardly noticed. He ate when they fed him and lay down when they told him to. He heard nothing, saw nothing except the girl. They had never told him her name and he needed none, knowing that names are used only to differentiate one person from another. For him, there were no other people, so there was no necessity for a name.

Her image was constantly before him. Sometimes she came before him in a sparkling shower of music that evaporated and died before she drew close. Sometimes she ran amidst the streaming colors of the wind, snatching a strip to bind the glory of her hair. Sometimes she stood in twilight, disappointed and forlorn, and the soul within Lang's body howled with grief that no one could ever again offer her kindness or comfort. He breathed only because, as long as he breathed, he could envision the miracle of her face.

The cruelty of her destruction made Whitley's soul weep, not for the girl, who could no longer remember it, but for himself, on whom she would never look with love, or even recognition. The cruelty of chance that had trapped his soul in the body of the man who had killed her was anguish past bearing.

Like a stench, his despair filled the cell and offended all who went near him. They did not leave him there many days. Two men came one morning and said they were taking him to a place for "psychiatric evaluation". He rose torpidly and went with them.

They were almost there. They were in sight of the white building, when a tire blew as they crossed a small bridge and one side of the car was crushed against the four-foot parapet. Gasoline trickled from the damaged tank and one of the men jerked the door open, saying, "Get out!"

The intensity of the pain in Whitley's soul invigorated the strong legs of the young body he had confiscated. He was out of the car and over the parapet before the car door was fully opened. He clasped his hands tightly behind him as he entered the river and his soul escaped, along with his breath, in a great up-rushing silvery bell.

Frank

Frank Tipton looked at his wife, sleeping in the frowzy bed, and barely restrained himself from waking her. He took her purse from the dresser and found her paycheck, which he placed on a card table alongside a much-handled deck of cards. He dug into the purse again and brought out the little zipper bag in which she kept her tips. Thirteen dollars! He was vaguely alarmed by the unlucky number and dismayed by the meagerness of the amount, although it was about average for a week-night at the "Come-on Inn," a mediocre restaurant and bar where she worked.

"Jillsey!" he yelled, and going to the bed, he grabbed both her wrists and jerked her into a sitting position. "Where's the rest of the money?" His wife stared at him dazed and terrified. Frank joggled her to bring her more fully awake. "I was in there last night and you were running your little ass off waiting on two big parties. Ten or twelve people to a table. Don't hold out on me!"

Comprehension washed over Jillsey's face. "I paid your dry cleaning bill. Around ten o'clock Rudin came in and asked me for it, right in front of the bartenders. You owed over two months." Tentatively, she tried to free her wrists.

Frank was pale with fury and disappointment. He let her go. "Get up," he said," and endorse the check. I want to get it cashed early so I'll have time for a nap before the game tonight." He gestured toward the check on the table. Moving like a somnambulist, Jillsey got out of bed and endorsed the check, with Frank looking over her shoulder. He folded the slip of blue paper and put it in his pocket. "You sneaky little bitch!" he said. "The cleaning! When you knew I needed every dime I can get for tonight's game!" He lifted a fist, longing to appease his anger by knocking his wife down.

"Don't do it, Frank," Jillsey said quietly. You know Mr. Bellardo won't let the girls work with marks all over them. He thinks it makes us look like prostitutes."

"We might be better off, if you were a prostitute," Frank answered. "You'd make more money in less time."

Jillsey's clear brown eyes were suddenly murky with shock and foreboding. "I don't suppose you gave the landlord the money I left for the rent."

In mimicry of her frightened tone, Frank said in a tiny voice, "No, I didn't give the landlord any money today, or last month either." He grinned and spoke normally. "The old letch comes in person to collect, hoping to see you, glamour-puss. He drools every time he mentions your name. We'd never have to pay rent again, if you'd be reasonable." He went to the dresser and began brushing his fair, delicate hair. He put lotion on his pudgy cheeks and drew a finger along his brows, light brown and dainty as a woman's. He gazed for a moment into the rather senseless soft, blue eyes reflected in the mirror. A choirboy, he thought. I look like a goddamned choirboy – who wouldn't dream of cheating at cards.

He had come back from the bank and been home quite a while before he noticed that Jillsey had changed. At first, he thought she was just huffy and giving him the silent treatment, but her silence was not the pent up, active silence of a woman who will not permit herself to speak. She seemed unaffected by his presence, remaining quiet because she had nothing whatever to say to him.

"Why don't you get some rest?" he asked eventually. It's a long time until two a.m."

Jillsey was mending the costume she wore at work, a brief gray dress with a flared shirt that showed white, ruffled panties below the hemline, making it at once demure and provocative. She was indifferent to his overture. "I'll be okay."

Frank turned to the mirror, so he didn't see Jillsey shake her head. He didn't hear her say to herself, "I thought when I married Frank that he would turn out better."

Frank undressed and tried to nap, while Jillsey bathed and wrote a letter, but he was perplexed by her attitude and unable to sleep. She was the one who had always made the first ingratiating remark, the one who wanted to smooth things over and who pretended to be happy. He got out of the bed and tried again. "I'll start dinner if you like."

Jillsey waved newly painted nails. "Not on my account. You know I can have all my meals at the restaurant. They're part of my salary and get deducted anyway. I buy groceries just because you want home cooked meals." She gathered up her gear and stowed it in the dresser. "But I'd better go a little early." She took fresh jeans and a blouse into the bathroom. When she came out, she was ready to leave, except for her costume, which she draped over her arm.

Strangely troubled, Frank put on a robe and followed her out onto the tiny porch of their cabin, one of twelve ratty little structures known as the "Twilight Motel – daily, weekly, monthly rates." It was getting dark as Jillsey passed under a light, Frank watched her brown hair swinging against her shoulders and her compact, curvaceous little figure moving jauntily toward the sidewalk. With stunning clarity, he understood what was bothering him. Jillsey could, without half trying, get herself another man any time she wanted to.

The minute the thought came to mind, he saw a male figure join Jillsey and walk her toward the blinking lights of the Come-on Inn. He ran to the sidewalk and watched, but couldn't really see the fellow, although Jillsey seemed clear enough. At any rate, the guy came out again right away. Frank immediately began to nurture a suspicion that they had made a date for later on. Across the street, a woman coming out of a motor court noticed Frank's robe and bare feet. She laughed and he hurried back inside.

That night he played poorly, so distracted that, once or twice, he misread his cards. The dim figure had been tall, hadn't it, and sort of graceful. You might say elegant. And it had bent toward Jillsey with flattering courtesy. Furthermore, Frank was fairly sure he'd seen the man before. Around two, when he'd lost everything except the thirteen dollars in tips, he threw in his hand. "Gotta go pick up my wife."

"That's a new twist," said an irritated player. "I've never known you to pick her up before."

A few yards from the Inn, Frank saw Jillsey and the stranger walking towards him. They strolled along in silence. In the early morning quiet, Frank could hear the faint scuffing of Jillsey's heels, but the man's feet, most likely shod in expensive shoes, made no sound. Jillsey yawned frequently. Her companion seemed to be wearing a hat of some kind that obscured his face. Damn the bastard! Frank thought, he knows how to keep himself from being recognized! He had meant to confront the pair when he caught them together, but there was something so innocuous in their manner they might have been two people who had accidently drawn abreast of each other on the street. Frank decided not to reveal himself. He let them pass and fall behind, watching their every move.

Suddenly, they were illuminated by a car turning out of the motor court. The man had removed his hat and his pale hair was haloed briefly by the headlights. He wore narrow trousers fitted to his slender legs and a full-skirted jacket that reached well below his buttocks. The hat he carried looked like a top hat. Frank grinned. An entertainer! One of the fancy dudes from the Inn dressed up like a riverboat gambler. Running on the balls of his feet, he closed the distance between himself and the sauntering couple, following them to the door of the shoddy little cabin. He had his key ready and the moment they closed the door he let himself in.

Jillsey was alone.

"Where is he?" Frank snarled. "Where's your song and dance man?" He charged around the small apartment, looking into the half empty closet, the shower stall and the miniscule kitchenette. The place had no back door. The windows were set above shoulder height and there was no place else to look. He swung around towards Jillsey, aching to beat an answer out of her, but she had taken a position in the bathroom doorway, ready to duck inside and lock herself in. "There's nobody here, Frank," she said, regarding him with disgust. "It's just somebody you dreamed up. I never saw him, myself."

"Liar!" Frank screamed. "Lying bitch!"

"You're so afraid of losing the money I bring in, you're scaring yourself to death," Jillsey said. "That man's your creation. If you saw him once, you can see him again. Look around."

Frank couldn't resist looking into the shadowy corner that had once been occupied by a broken luggage rack. There was certainly something there. A man-shaped something that grew steadily clearer and more solid until Frank knew what he was going to see: the man he would have been, if he hadn't been born a scared rabbit with a mean streak in him, his secret dream self. He gazed, entranced, at his fair-haired twin, four inches taller and thirty pounds lighter. Lean, keen and invincible with a haughty, reckless face and compelling sapphire eyes, no wonder he seemed familiar. The man smiled at Frank with mingled charm and conscious superiority and Frank almost wilted with pleasure. His visitor wore high-waisted fawn trousers, a rust colored coat and a paisley cravat tucked into a vest of olive-green brocade. As he offered his hand to the smiling man, Frank noticed there were no buttons on the vest. Immediately, a row of faceted jet buttons glittered against the green silk.

They went at once to the card table and sat down. With a languid hand, the stranger invited Frank to pick up the soiled cards. From an inner pocket, he took a sheaf of bills. Frank, shuffling expertly, said, "I guess we both know what we're playing for."

His companion gave Frank a long, silent look. "Are you sure that's what you want?" Frank nodded and placed the shuffled cards in the center of the table.

He saw Jillsey dart out of the bathroom and pick up the cards. He yelled, "Hey!" and grabbed at the deck, but Jillsey laid it aside and said, "Frank, listen a minute!" He ignored her, his eyes on the face of his almost twin, who seemed faintly amused and more than faintly bored.

He felt the heel of Jillsey's hand under his chin, forcing his head back so he was obliged to look at her. "Whadda you want, Jillsey?"

"Is he here? Are you gambling with him?"

"Of course, you nit wit."

"What are the stakes?"

Frank put both hands around Jillsey's waist and dug his thumbs cruelly into the flesh above her hip bones. "Get away from me, Jillsey!"

She endured, maintaining the pressure on his chin. "What are the stakes?"

"If I win, I keep my life and get his looks and personality. If he wins, he keeps his looks and personality and gets my life."

"Who is he?"

Frank laughed. "He's me! A bigger, handsomer, smarter me!"

Jillsey rocked his head from side to side as though trying to shake some sense into it. "This is all imaginary, Frank. If you win his good looks, or whatever it is you want, it will be only an imaginary gain. If he wins, your life could become only an imaginary life. It's crazy and dangerous!" She let go of his chin and stepped away from him.

Franks hand pounced on the cards. "You're wrong, Jillsey! It's a paradox. The winner is the same man, whether I become him or he becomes me. The winner's the winner and the loser's the winner. Don't you see?" He reshuffled the cards, and again, placed them in the center of the table.

"Sort of," Jillsey said. She touched his heated face. "I wish I could care more, Frank, but I don't really give a damn what you do. I'm going to bed."

Frank found that playing a crafty game and keeping the image of his dream-self intact took a prodigious amount of concentration. Whenever he gave his attention to his hand, the beautiful image began to waver in and out of existence. Whenever he gave his full attention to his opponent, the man gamed with a heartless expertise that was depressing. Frank held on to the thought that it made sense for his better self to be a better player.

When daylight came, Frank, trembling and breathing hard, was devastated by fatigue. The man shuffled the cards and dealt two. Frank knew it was his last hand. He picked it up and his heart sank into his shoes when he saw it was the two of clubs and the seven of diamonds. He had nowhere to go with that, no straight draw, no flush draw.

The man smiled. For the first time, he seemed fully solid and present. "Ready to fold, Frank?"

Frank was startled to realize that the man really wasn't imaginary. He was almost relieved when he set the cards down and said, "I suppose you will take over my life, now."

The man smiled wider, and said "Frank, I never said I was your better self. I didn't name the stakes."

"You can call me Hubert Vanderpool. Hubert was a Mississippi gambler, who's been dead a long time, but he gets restless sometimes without a pack of cards in his hands. I brought Hubert along just for you."

Frank was so tired that he could hardly think straight. He fumbled through what he had lost. "What about Jillsey?" he asked the man, still sitting there with that unsettling half smile.

"Hubert likes a pretty girl. He went with her to the Inn and back. You were right about that. He saw the costume over her arm and thought she might lead him to a place with "gaming rooms."

Jillsey slept soundly and late. When she got up, Frank was sitting stone cold dead at the card table. The thirteen unlucky dollars were lying among the scattered cards and under his hand was a sheet of paper that read:

Jillsey,

I played too hard and got too tired. Something broke and my life is draining out of me like sand through a hole in a sack. I thought of waking you but, after missing out on being what I always wanted to be—I just don't give a damn what happens to me. I suppose I should be sorry for the way I treated you, but that's not my style.

Frank

P.S. Hubert's coming back tonight for another game. Can you get us a fresh deck of cards?

Jillsey took the thirteen dollars off the table and put it in her purse. Then she packed her suitcase. The last thing that she put in it was the grey costume with the ruffled white panties.

Street Car Winter

Once, I had a brief bout of the flu in a grievous Chicago winter, when hundreds of truckloads of filthy snow had been dumped along the shore and even out onto the ice of frozen Lake Michigan. Safety lines had been strung along the bridges to keep people from being bulldozed into the traffic by the avalanche of wind that poured down the canal and the river. It was the year that, on the north side of the streets, snow lay heaped next to the sidewalks for ninety days, growing blacker each day from coal smoke and freshened each morning with a cleaner stratum spewed along the top by snow plows.

My son was in school in Mexico City and my daughter, left pale and puckish by a series of colds, had accompanied her father to Florida, where he worked during the winters.

I had looked forward to living alone for a while, freed from the necessity of contributing to anyone else's comfort. I planned to do a certain amount of the cleaning, sorting and discarding that are mandatory, if apartment dwellers are to live in any degree of order. For a year, or more, I had been compiling a list of books I wanted to read when I had the leisure. I meant to see a couple of operas or ballets with friends. But I went to bed almost as soon as husband and daughter were out the door.

I don't remember being particularly ill and, except for some rather remarkable fever dreams, went through the usual aspirin, fluids and bed rest routine with the usual results and returned to the office in a few days. When I came home from my first day back at work, depression, black, hideous and forever hopeless, struck me like sudden insanity and, to the witless despair that suffocated me was added the fear that the mild disease had damaged my brain.

That evening I sat for an hour, despondent and trying now and again to have a good cry, thinking it would ease the dementia that immobilized me. The seizure, however, lacked any element of self-pity and tears seemed frivolous in view of my stark evaluation of a life raped of all solace. I could readily have believed that I was possessed by a monstrous, un-glad, spirit and that my soul had died.

"Look, lady, I scolded myself, all you'll get sitting here is a square bottom. Get out of here. You're bound to see something or someone that'll make you forget your misery. No, don't run to friends. Sympathy is the last thing you need." To my dismay, I found that, like a recalcitrant Lazarus, I wanted to remain huddled in my lightless tomb.

By applying a degree of self-discipline never before exerted, I put on extra socks, boots, a thick sweater under my coat and a pair of my daughter's woolen pants in an eye-catching plaid. They were too short for me and slipped out of my boot tops when I stepped up into the streetcar.

The car was packed with mourners and corpses. It was impossible to tell which was which. Each sat sheathed in a cocoon of privacy, as though enclosed in a visible plastic baggie. No one spoke a word, except a drunken buffoon, who worked his way up the crowded aisle, asking everyone the time. He had his hat on upside down. The crown was crushed over his greasy hair and the brim stood out around his skull in a warped halo of dirty, brown felt. His overcoat was wrong side out. The sleeves were lined in a striped material that resembled pillow ticking. No one would tell him the time. Each sterile wrapped passenger he approached slid an unseeing glance away from him, as if drunkenness might be contagious through eye contact. When he reached me, I looked at my watch and told him it was seven-ten. His bristly cheeks bunched in a delighted grin and he hitched up the sopping cuff of his pants to reveal a wristwatch strapped around his ankle. "That's right," he agreed happily. "ten after seven." That was all the poor fool wanted: a chance to display his watch on his ankle.

"I been on a three-day bender," he told me, snickering. "My wife's gonna' kill me when I get home." He fished around clumsily in a pocket of his inside-out coat and brought forth a flat pint bottle made of brown glass. "You wanna' drink?" "Save it," I advised him. "You're going to need some hair for dog-bite in the morning." He nodded in agreement and put the bottle away. I hoped his wife wouldn't pour his hooch down the drain during the night.

I got out of the car at Wabash and Adams. It was darkish under the El tracks and there was little to entice pedestrians to the area. As I moved north to a more populous neighborhood, a slender young Negro man wavered toward me. His afro hairdo was bleached and gorgeous, golden blond and he wore a glistening white leather jacket. He couldn't have been more than nineteen, perhaps much less than that, but his dark young face had already been made repulsive by years of debauchery. As I watched, he threw an arm around a lamppost and vomited into the gutter.

The falling snow was fine as salt, too dry to pack down. It squeaked underfoot and felt more like sand than snow. A couple of blocks past Wabash, I stopped before a large florist's window crowded with rows, ranks and clusters of sweet, small tulips, all of them the yellow color of daffodils, of forsythia, of spring. The floor of the window was covered deeply with a white, granular substance that duplicated the snow and enhanced the illusion of a magical garden in the midst of winter-cursed Chicago. They must have sold a thousand pots of those sunny little plants.

I continued my therapeutic excursions, starting, always, from my apartment. My mental disorder was like an ill-natured dog that was left at home during the day. I think I must have performed adequately at the office, though perhaps, without flair. I can remember no single incident to give me a clue. In the evenings I went home for the ill-natured dog, to make certain he came with me. I dared not go adventuring directly from work, lest he should be waiting to attack me at home when I got back.

I thought frequently of suicide at this time, much as I thought of learning to cook, or of having my nose remodeled. The idea was most inviting, but was not a thing I could seriously plan on doing. The expenditure of emotional energy required to overcome my inertia left me exhausted, but every evening I dragged myself out of the tar pit, bundled up warmly and started out. The prospect of sitting in a darkened movie made me uneasy and I was disinclined to spend time with people who had a right to ride the street cars to the Loop.

On one occasion, I very nearly lost all the ground I had gained. I took a bus to the northwest side of town. As usual, the vehicle was jammed. This crowd was very noisy and very talkative. On all sides of me, voices rose in unintelligible conversation. I could identify some of the Poles by their heavy bone structure and dense-looking complexions. Even the ones who weren't very big had a massive look about them. The girls had beautiful, rounded calves and thick ankles. I could hear scraps of talk in Yiddish and Lithuanian. Two Italian men played chess on a magnetic board. Eight or ten lively, gabbling people seemed to belong together in a group, but I couldn't recognize their language. I heard not one word of English and began to realize I was a pitiful minority of one.

At a corner stop, a man handed two stringy teen-age girls into the bus. They were obviously the usual English-Irish-and-something-else mixture from whom one expects to hear English crudely spoken. I edged closer to them like an exile longing to hear the speech of home. They began talking at once – in sign language.

Only a few people, besides the teenagers left the bus before we reached the end of the line in a neighborhood of high, narrow houses set close against each other on a long, dim street. The only sign of life was a lighted tavern called "Josephine's" from which the rollicking racket of a polka came in gusts as the passengers left the bus and went inside.

I went with them. I couldn't have felt less at home in a native cantina in Mexico, or a tea house in Japan. Every record in the jukebox was a polka. Couples began skipping and whirling in a floor-shaking dance as soon as drinks were ordered. I had been watching them for ten or fifteen minutes, when it became clear that the clientele of the place was a small, stratified society. I could sense friendships, jealousies and, among the men, irritating rivalries for un-guessable positions. The women behaved oddly, in accordance with a ritual of right conduct having to do, I surmised, with who was tough enough to prevent encroachment on staked-out territory. The two or three women who did not monitor their behavior in the same way seemed to be fair game for any man in the place who hadn't brought his wife along.

A number of the customers looked at me with a modicum of welcome and a great deal of speculation, but something in their social code prevented their speaking to me and I wasn't about to shatter any taboos by speaking first.

When I ordered my obligatory beer from Josephine, (a stunning black-eyed Greek) I learned that the lively group from the bus belonged to a Ukrainian marching society. Her Polish husband gave me some pretzels to munch with the beer while I waited for the next bus home.

I began carrying a small notebook in my purse. I had no ambition to be a poet, but I enjoyed writing rhymed verse and sometimes composed a very satisfying kind of doggerel on the streetcar. My bleak mood was so much lightened by this exercise that I was able to remain comfortably home on Sundays, writing verse, instead of risking frostbite by prowling the Loop in search of the occasional fruit market, curio shop, or bookstall open on the conventional day of rest.

Most of my little notebooks have, mercifully, been lost. Every verse written in that time reflected my somber frame of mind, being composed, without exception, in that dullest of all forms, iambic tetrameter. My hold on regained optimism was fragile, but one dismal evening, when sleet abraded the windows and the interior of the streetcar reeked with the doggy smell of wet wool, I wrote:

> Help! Save me from the four-foot line!
> I fear the ugly tetra ped,
> Who paces every thought of mine
> With hateful, even, metric tread.

> I slyly shift from foot to foot
> Within the short diameter
> Of his patrol, lest he should put
> A hex on my pentameter
>
> He scans with pale, iambic eyes
> Each subterfuge, each weak design
> Planned to encompass his demise.
> I'm no match for that four-foot line.
>
> Had I but wit enough and rhyme,
> With words as sharp as scimitars
> I'd make short work of F.F. Line.
> I'd chop him down to de-meters!

Having broken the spell of the four-foot line with this dizzy incantation, I started a science fiction story about a writer who rescues an albino midget during a storm and keeps her as a captive source of inspiration. I worked on this piece intermittently for a few weeks. Then, I picked up a magazine from a newsstand and found a tale about an albino midget. Without a trace of depression, I consigned my midget to her hometown on Alpha Centauri and began a story about a farmer, who incubates and hatches a clutch of angel's eggs. I was no longer threatened by the ill-natured dog of melancholy, and I abandoned my evening excursions on the streetcars. Instead, I hurried home to my farmer.

I wrote at the same table where I had my morning egg and coffee. When my gingham placemat became too messy to write on, I laid a clean one over it and got on with my story. In early March, my daughter came home without warning. In some embarrassment, I tried to remove the accumulation of place mats and they came up in a solid block of fifteen or so.

Bulging packets of outdated bills, receipts and correspondence still lay in drawers, their edges curled in strangulation by rubber bands. Dressers were still crammed with mate-less socks and undergarments dead of fatigue. The clothes closets were a scandal and it was snowing again.

I never tried, really, to explain what I had done with my winter, especially since nobody asked me for an explanation. Privately, I managed to get myself down, alive, from the cross, but this notion seemed a little too flamboyant to confide to anyone. It was months before I learned that extreme depression was a common aftermath of the influenza going around that year.

The day my daughter came home, or one day soon after, we bought a potted tulip. Not one of the miraculous little yellow ones of midwinter, but a lusty red token of spring. The inside of the petals was marked with spear-shaped smudges of velvety black around the stamen, so that, when you looked directly into the scarlet cup, you could see the secret black flower within the red one.

Summer Television

Maggie Ryan spread deviled ham on crackers, piled them on a paper plate and, picking up a cup of rum laced with cold tea, she moved into her living room and sat down in a rocking chair that faced the television, which wasn't plugged into the outlet.

The chair was large, but her abundant figure sagged over it in ungraceful loops wherever the structure of the chair permitted. The day was warm and Maggie, who despised panty hose, had shoved her stockings down so that they hung around her shins like loose, crumpled collars. With a contented sigh, she put her feet on a ruptured ottoman and pulled her flimsy skirt well above her knees for coolness. While she ate her lunch, she regarded the flaccid, curdled flesh of her thighs with disgust and forgiveness.

Before she started on her tea, she looked at the yellow-faced mantel clock and decided it was unlikely that her daughter would drop in at eleven-thirty in the forenoon. The girl visited her about once a month, but she never telephoned in advance and Maggie was always nervous that today might be the day her daughter would come by and see in careless housekeeping an indication that her mother was unwell.

"I'm fine." Maggie said aloud. "I feel great. Except for being short-winded most of the time, I'm as good as new. When it gets cooler, I'll start taking long walks and shuck a few pounds." She sipped from the cup and, rocking happily, stared at the television set.

The picture that appeared was exquisitely colored and three-dimensional. She saw herself walking down a woodland path towards Lydia's red house glowing among the trees. It was blessedly cool here and something invisible sifted down from the trees that was part perfume, part stimulant and part bliss. She could tell that the flowers and little islands of grass beside the path weren't real. They were painted, or woven into a carpet, but they were so beautiful it made no difference to her. They'll never, never, wither, she thought. The bird sounds seemed real enough.

She moved easily along the path, delighted to see that, as usual, she was sixty pounds lighter here in the forest. The stiffness was gone from her knees. And her feet felt slender and flexible.

"Hey!" she yelled at the figure in the box and the miniature Maggie turned and looked at her. She was pleased to see that she hadn't become young. The rich black hair was still chalk marked with white and her face was a thinner version of the fifty-five year old face she wore every day. More vital of course. More vivid in a way that made her best features show up better.

I wouldn't want to be young again, she thought, as the Maggie image turned and walked on. Young like some of today's poets and painters and actors, maybe, but not young like I was. For me, being young was all pain and awkwardness and embarrassment. I was self-conscious and sick with longings for things I couldn't identify. An impossible girl! A ridiculous, unhappy girl! I'm glad she's gone.

"Wait a minute!" Maggie called, and the television obediently froze, but the birds sang on and a sighful breeze fanned the painted glade. After she returned with a fresh cup of rum and tea, a man walked onto the margin of the path and waited for Maggie to come even with him.

Manfred! She thought. Where in hell did he get a name like Manfred? But she was happy to see him just the same. Some days he didn't appear. From this distance he looked like the handsomest man in the world gone a little bit to seed.

Up close, he looked the same. Her gaze explored the tanned face, the sweet mouth with curly corners and the peaked, slightly sinister eyebrows. Laughter lines radiated from eyes the color of wet asphalt. The dimples of boyhood had degenerated into humorous creases down his cheeks. He had a budding paunch. With joy and an utter trust that she had never been able to feel for any other man, Maggie put her arms around Manfred's neck. He clasped her affectionately and gave her a kiss that was loving, but lacked fire. "How are you, Pegeen?" He examined her face with a tender regard. His touch seemed intentionally intimate as he laced his fingers through hers and swung her hand as they continued down the path.

"Marvelous," Maggie answered. "It's good to see you, Manfred. I'm on my way to Lydia's." Exasperating bastard, she thought. He's either so polite and gentlemanly he's scared to death of offending me, or else he's a eunuch. I wish I could do like the girls in the movies and just ask him, plain and simple, if he wants to take me to bed. But I haven't got the nerve. Maybe if he were more flamboyant and sinful, I could heat up his blood a little. He looks like he's just made for sinful women.

Her dissatisfaction evaporated and she squeezed Manfred's hand, quickened her pace and hummed MacNamara's Band as they marched up to Lydia's house. There was a knocker on the door, a bronze lion's head holding a big ring in its teeth, and Maggie enthusiastically slammed the ring against the wood while she called, "Lydia! It's me, Maggie. Can I come in?"

Her question was echoed by another voice, "Can I come in?" and Maggie jerked her attention from the television in time to keep from spilling the contents of her sagging cup into her lap. She drew a deep breath, rubbed her eyes with her free hand and said, "Of course you can, Sheila. Come in, love."

Sheila Radulovic stumbled into the room. "Good lord, Mother, it's dark as a cave in here. Why are all the blinds down?" She went to a window, opened the drapes and raised the shabby blind. "Oh God!" Mother, you're not sick, are you?"

"Of course not. Don't be such a worrywart. Where's little Roger?"

"I left him with a neighbor. She owes me. What are you drinking?"

"Tea. Let me get you some."

"Tea? Mother, I could smell liquor as soon as I came through the door."

Maggie chuckled. "Well, dear heart, there's some tea in the cup too."

Sheila removed the shrouds from the only other window in the room. She came back, brushing her hands against each other to rid them of dust, and stood looking at the rum bottle on the table. "That's expensive stuff for a woman like you who has practically no income."

"It surely is," Maggie agreed, "but I don't really buy an awful lot of it."

Sheila began to cry and fell into a chair near her mother's. "I know you don't. I'm being nasty because I'm worried sick. I don't know what we're going to do. I especially don't know what you're going to do." She seemed shattered by despair and wept without making any effort to control her tears. Maggie went into the kitchen and poured some tea into a mug, which she brought into the living room along with a clean dishtowel. She topped off the cup with rum and held out cloth and cup to her daughter. "Dry your eyes, dear, and have some tea. Tell me why you're in such a tizzy."

Sheila blotted her eyes, sipped from her cup and said, "That's what I came here for, so I'd better get it done. Savo got laid off from his job four weeks ago. I didn't tell you because he said he'd be able to get another job without any trouble. But he couldn't and he didn't. He tried to get a loan on the house, but without a job, he couldn't swing that either. As a last-ditch effort, he tried to get a loan on his life insurance, but there's a clause in the policy that prohibits that kind of thing. So, the money I've been skimming from the household accounts and giving to you can't be skimmed anymore." For a moment, it seemed that Sheila might succumb to another crying fit, but she sipped from her cup and unfolded the dishtowel, which was a thing of considerable dimensions. She grinned at her mother. "I could, at least, have had the foresight to bring my own Kleenex."

In the strong light coming from the breached windows, Maggie could see that her child had been crying before she arrived, perhaps off and on for days. Her eyelids were thick and red. Her rather delicate nose was a roughened, hot pink. Even her mouth was puffy and chapped. On one cheekbone was a dark bruise from which the concealing makeup was scaling away.

Maggie looked Sheila in the eye. "Savo's got a short temper, a hard fist and a mean mouth. I'd guess that he didn't get laid off. He got fired and can't get a recommendation sent to a new employer. This is the umpteenth time it's happened. I don't know why you lie to make him look good. You know nothing can do that."

Sheila sighed. "I don't lie to make him look better. I lie to make me look better. I can't stand having people wonder why I stay married to him."

"Why do you?"

"Because I'm used to him, I guess. And, generally, he doesn't bother me much. He goes to work, comes home and eats, and goes out again. We don't... he hasn't asked me to make love for months."

"When that happened between me and your father, it was because he'd taken up with another woman."

Sheila looked at her mother in pink-eyed, blinking surprise. "Daddy did that?"

"Oh yes, Daddy did that. She was a prim, strait-laced, mousy, little widow and I never knew what attraction she had for him. The truth is, I was relieved. Your daddy was raised by a mother who'd gone bilious on a surfeit of religion. By the time I got to him, he was ruined. At bedtime, he always approached me with a mixture of lechery and shame, as if he were about to wallow in obscenity. Maybe the widow felt the same way about sex. If I'd had a private income, she could have kept him forever."

"But she didn't," Sheila said. "Why not?"

"One month, I paid the bills and all the checks bounced. So, I bundled up his dirty laundry and his dry cleaning and the bouncy checks and the unpaid bills and sent them to her house, addressed to his attention. I figured if all the money was going to her place, then that was the place for the expenses to go." Maggie sighed. "His turtledove sent him home. Neither your father or I ever mentioned her again."

Sheila said in a clipped, careful way that conveyed her outrage more clearly than shouting could ever do, "Savo's lady isn't meek and mousy. She's a trash bag. She's tough and wild and extravagant. When Savo lost his job, I went to the bank to see if we had the money for him to go back to school and learn a skill. He can't be a stock clerk all his life. These days there are fewer and fewer jobs for stock clerks. At the bank they told me he'd drawn out all our savings! I'd divorce him, if I had courage, but I know he'd beat me up if I tried it."

"Have you thought of going back to work, yourself?"

"Of course, I have!" Sheila touched her bruised cheek. "That's how I got this. Savo wants me to stay at home and take care of Roger, even if we starve to death while I'm doing it." She hammered her knees in frustration. " I called Harrison-Hardway and asked if I could have my old job back. They were pleased to hear from me and said come right in, but Savo says no wife of his is going to work. Mother what can we do? If my husband were halfway human, you could live with us and look after Roger while I worked and Savo went back to school."

"That'll be the day," Maggie said airily. She went into the kitchen, her stockings dragging over her shoe heels and came back with paper plates loaded with chicken salad, sliced tomatoes and crackers. Sheila was in the bathroom. The apartment was so small Maggie could smell the witch hazel her daughter was applying to her damaged face.

"How much is Savo's insurance?" Maggie asked.

From the bathroom, Sheila answered, "Twenty-five thousand, but we can't do anything with that." She came into the room and picked up her plate. "I told you, Savo tried."

"One thing you can do is keep the premiums up, in case his girlfriend gets drunk and shoots him." Maggie reached into her voluminous brassiere and brought out some bills, folded and fastened with a paper clip. She tossed the money into Sheila's lap. "There's a couple hundred there. Be sure you pay the premiums."

"Mother, where did you get this?"

"You might say I got it from Lydia. I'm lucky. I won a number game that was running in the newspaper. I've been lucky ever since Lydia gave me this." Maggie took hold of a thin cord that lay around her neck and drew out a small cloth bag. "A toby, she called it. Cheer up, love. My luck is your luck."

"I remember Lydia," Sheila said. She was that old black woman you were such pals with. You mean you've been wearing that bag ever since she left? It must be ten years. I remember the day you said she'd gone away. Daddy had just died and you cried for a week. I couldn't tell which one of them you were grieving for."

"It's been twelve years," Maggie said, "and she wasn't all that black, more of a citron color."

"Well, I never saw her. You always had her at the house when you were alone, but I thought you said she was black and nearly a hundred years old. After all, twelve years ago, I was still in school."

Maggie stroked the toby. "She was the kindest, the wisest, the most interesting friend anyone could have. After Lydia, I never found anyone I wanted to be friends with." She held up the little bag. "I put clean covers over it every once in a while. How do you like this paisley material? Lydia used to tell my fortune and, no matter how scary the cards were, she managed to read them in such a way that nothing really bad could happen to me. She could do horoscopes too."

Sheila was clasping and unclasping her hands, not quite wringing them. "Mother, if only you could come and stay with me! I'd see to it that you got out more and made some new friends. You're still young and it's bad for you to sit here, tippling in a dark room. It's morbid. If Lydia isn't actually defunct, she's at least a hundred and twelve and, obviously, not of a mind to play with fortune cards at this point."

"More like two-thousand years old," Maggie said. Her teacup had been miraculously refilled and she was swinging gaily in her rocker. "Said her father was a student of the Scriptures and named her for the woman who befriended Paul and Silas in Macedonia. She was a seller of purple."

"Purple?"

"Costly stuff in those days. The Macedonian Lydia was probably a good business woman and quite wealthy." Maggie smiled at the ceiling gliding back and forth above her. "Personally, I never liked Saint Paul very much. I got the notion that he detested women. Always using them and belittling them."

She giggled. "He thought widows shouldn't be allowed to drink wine."

"Oh, for Pete's sake, Mother! What's Saint Paul got to do with your Lydia being two thousand years old?"

"It was the prayer meeting. I looked Lydia up in the New Testament and, while Paul was sheltering in her house, he went to a place where prayer service was commonly held in the open air. I suppose Lydia went along, since Paul was a stranger in that place and she was his sponsor. At any rate, I got the impression there was a fairly large crowd and among them was a young girl who had the gift of soothsaying. She kept shouting that Saint Paul's spiritual message was true. You'd think he'd be glad of her support, but the arrogant old preacher was annoyed and exorcised her spirit of clairvoyance. I don't think he asked the girl's permission."

Sheila glanced at the rum bottle and was relieved to find that it was empty. "I see," she said, but her voice sounded befuddled.

"No, you don't see," her mother laughed. "The thing is, nobody said what became of the clairvoyant spirit that was taken from the girl. I think it went into Lydia of Macedonia and that it's with her still. I'm sure that Saint Paul's Lydia and my Lydia are one and the same." Maggie noted the distress in her daughter's face and added quickly "and don't think for a minute I'm going to tell this to anyone but you."

"If you want to rewrite the Scriptures to keep your friend alive forever, I don't see any real harm in it. Perhaps some potted plants would be a good idea. You'd have to leave your windows clear so the plants could get air and sun." Sheila stroked her mother's arm and kissed her cheek. "I feel braver than when I got here. You've helped a lot. Thanks for the money. I don't know when I can return it. If you really are lucky, you'd better play another newspaper game." She moved towards the door. "See you," she said.

"Call first!" Maggie yelled after her.

For a while, Maggie rocked and hummed, reliving the hours of her friendship with Lydia as if she were inhaling the aroma of dried flowers. Eventually, she slept. When she awoke, it was dark. "Thank God, Sheila opened the blinds," she muttered as she wandered clumsily into the bathroom. "Otherwise it would be as black in here as the inside of a cow." She turned on the light, washed her face, brushed her hair and chewed up a Cloret. Then she went back to her chair and sat down, leaving the room illuminated only by the light from the half-open bathroom door.

She had never tried watching her television in the dark, but she stared at the murky screen to see what would happen and, presently, she saw herself walking down the path in brilliant moonlight. It was wonderful! The night smells were more mysterious than the daytime smells and, when she extended her bare arms in the moonlight, they looked as white and smooth as marble.

Lydia's door shone dimly red as Maggie lifted and dropped the knocker. Lydia opened the door and drew Maggie into a warm, candle-lit room. The two friends hugged each other and gossiped as if they hadn't met in a year, although it had been nothing like that long. They talked all night and the windows were just beginning to show as watery gray rectangles when Maggie said, "You know, of course that I've come to you about Sheila." She looked carefully at Lydia to assess the possibility of aid.

The old woman was fragile to the point of weightlessness. Seemingly, she was compounded of air, color and power. The irises of her black eyes were so large they filled the eye socket like the eyes of a deer. She had pushed the snowy cloud of her hair under a little beaded cap and, in the soft light her face was calm and kind. To the doting Maggie she appeared to be an ethereal Kwan Yin worked in amber. "Nothing for yourself?" she asked, as if coaxing Maggie to think of something she wanted.

"Well," Maggie said, "you already know my views on living in the house with children and grandchildren. Besides, I'd miss a lot of my television…programs…if Sheila gets her way."

Lydia nodded. "Give me the toby."

With some misgiving, Maggie removed the bag from her neck. "You'll give it back, won't you? I feel naked without it. And sort of vulnerable."

"Of course," Lydia assured her. The old lady thumbed through a sheaf of papers tied together with a thong that passed through two holes in the top of each page. When she found what she wanted, she took scissors and cut a strip of parchment from the page, rolled it into a tiny cylinder and put it into the bag. She handed the toby back to Maggie. "You're tired, dear friend. You should go home now."

Maggie barely remembered getting home. The moon was down and the path under the trees was dim, although their trunks showed black against the pallid intimation of daybreak. She struggled out of her chair and went to bed. She slept most of the day.

During the next two or three weeks, Maggie had the feeling that time had stopped and that Monday's events were repeated on Tuesday and Wednesday and on the next day, so that she lost count of the days of the week. Whenever she talked to her daughter on the phone, Sheila's voice always conveyed the same patient endurance. The situation was unchanged: Sheila and little Roger were living virtually alone. Savo was invariably vile tempered and depressed whenever he came home. They were getting by, for the moment, on Savo's unemployment insurance.

In Maggie's apartment, the tired faced clock seemed to be stuck forever at eleven thirty in the forenoon. She went daily to the woodland in her television set, but she never went to Lydia's house for fear her friend would think she was clamoring for more decisive results. The painted flowers along the path never grew or wilted and Manfred never came to meet her.

One morning, Maggie, feeling not so sprightly today, sauntered down the path and was totally surprised to see Manfred hurrying toward her. His embrace was ardent, his kiss offered her all the love of his passionate heart, his hands touched her face and bosom with gentle eagerness. She thought she might drop dead from ecstasy as she returned his embrace, his kiss, his touch.

They went among the trees to a little pavilion hung with chiming wind bells. Happy laughter spilled from Maggie's mouth as her lover unbuttoned her blouse. "I thought you could love only a sinful woman, Manfred. I'm glad I was wrong."

Manfred twined his arms around her bare waist and smiled into her eyes. "But, Pegeen, don't you know? You are sinful! You're a wicked, sinful woman." He kissed her again and they clung together while the moving branches scraped the roof of the pavilion, the birds warbled and the wind bells rang and rang. "I could do without those confounded chimes," Maggie grumbled as she surged out of her rocker and answered the phone.

"Mother? Oh Lord! Mother?"

Maggie was groggy and irritable. "What is it, Sheila?" She could hear a faint sound that made her think Sheila's teeth might be chattering. She pulled herself together. "What's the trouble, baby?"

"Mother, the police were just here. Savo and his girlfriend were at her place drinking and quarreling all night. By ten o'clock this morning they were both crazy drunk and savage as bobcats. And, Mother?"

"Yes, Sheila?"

"She took her gun and shot him twice in the face. Her name is Angelica. Like the candied stuff in fruitcake."

"Well, Sheila, I don't suppose you expect me to go all smarmy and offer you my insincere condolences."

"No. But I expect you to think about coming here to live. It will be much better for you than living in that terrible little apartment."

I can't do that, love." Maggie, with the telephone to her ear, turned to the television set. Manfred was dithering on the pathway, making urgent signals for her to come to him. "I won't be spending much time in this apartment," she told Sheila. "There's lots of summer left and you know what hot weather does to me. I've found a breezy cottage in the woods where I can go as often as I like. I was just going there now."

"But, Mother! Roger …"

"I'll get thin!" Maggie sang. "So thin a man can reach around me without using both arms."

"Listen, Mother. Roger and I need you."

"No, you don't. Your horoscope says you're going to make a happy marriage within the year."

"You're just saying that, trying to sidetrack me."

"It's absolutely true, Sheila. Trust me."

Sheila's voice sounded belligerent. "Even if it is true, you can't stay alone in some isolated house out in the wilderness. You've lost your mind!"

"I won't be alone very much, dear. You wanted me to make new friends? Well, this cottage has the friendliest neighbor." Maggie blew a kiss to the impatient Manfred.

Acknowledgments

Many thanks to all those who helped create this collection of stories by a once Texas girl who triumphed amidst the adversity that was the 20th century. Thank you to Kiki Cardarelli, Brendan Clark, and Celt Schira.

CPSIA information can be obtained
at www.ICGtesting.com
Printed in the USA
BVHW032018290121
R11801500001B/R118015PG598625BVX00004B/1